A T
Al

BY
VICTORIA GORDON

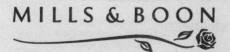

MILLS & BOON

MILLS & BOON LIMITED
ETON HOUSE, 18-24 PARADISE ROAD
RICHMOND, SURREY TW9 1SR

This for ROB BURR...

Who could never qualify as a heroine, even
under the most taxing circumstances.
But helped immensely.

*First published in Great Britain 1993
by Mills & Boon Limited*

© Victoria Gordon 1993

*Australian copyright 1993
Philippine copyright 1994
This edition 1994*

ISBN 0 263 78309 X

*Set in Times Roman 10½ on 12 pt.
91-9402-53120 C*

Made and printed in Great Britain

CHAPTER ONE

VASHTI stretched her throat as if for the sacrificial knife as she tipped her head back and stared upwards to an unseen heaven.

'But why *me*?' she asked, directing the question not at her immediate superior, who had provoked it, but past him, above him, to the nameless, invisible deity she half expected to reply in a barrage of thunderbolts.

'Because it was *you* that he asked for,' was the reply, but it came, of course, from Ross Chandler, whose rotund figure was all too visible, its Buddha-like attitude of benignity offset by eyes that never smiled, perhaps never had.

'And,' he continued with an attitude to match, 'since he apparently has friends in high places, it would be best to...'

His gesture upwards had vastly different overtones than had Vashti's. To Chandler, the only deity that existed was the Australian Taxation Office for which they both worked; the Commissioner for Taxation was the ultimate authority.

'But it doesn't make any sense,' Vashti argued. 'I don't know the first thing about writing, and certainly I'm no authority on the ways in which this office works. I'm just a field auditor. Surely there are people far better qualified for... for whatever this person wants.'

'He wants *you*. He is apparently writing a book in which the workings of the taxation office—and particularly the field audit side—play some significant role, and he wants someone he can consult regularly to ensure accuracy.' Her boss was unmoved by her concern. The request had been ratified from above, therefore she would follow through to the best of her ability. Or *he* would know the reason why.

'But that's just the point,' Vashti insisted. 'Why *me*? Surely there are much better people in this office to help Mr...?'

'Keene,' her boss supplied the name, through hardly moving lips. Vashti added his first name, but her own lips trembled noticeably, at least to herself.

'Phelan. Phelan Keene,' she whispered, shaking her mane of ash-blonde hair and clenching her teeth around the name as if to somehow subdue the memory it carried. 'Of course... of course it would be.'

And just knowing the name answered, at least in part, the manifold question of why. Vashti had spent the months just prior to his father's death working on a terribly convoluted—and still not complete—field audit on the family's wide-ranging Tasmanian business dealings. Phelan Keene hadn't been involved, except as a remote and distant partner in the overall scheme of things; he was a writer who spent virtually none of his time involved with the family's rural affairs. He'd only come home, she thought, for the funeral.

She narrowed her usually wide pale grey eyes and pushed time back a fortnight, back to a grave site...

The funeral for old Bede Keene had been held on a bleak Tuesday morning, the setting a tiny church that crouched on a high and windy ridge back in the hills behind Ouse. Once there'd been a settlement there, now there were a few isolated homesteads and a sign at the gravel-road junction. The aged church, refurbished in a dress of cream-coloured galvanised iron with a fresh-painted green roof, hunched in one corner of a small cemetery, as lonely as its setting. Many of the graves dated back to before 1900; some delineated entire family histories, and several were no more than humps in the ground, unmarked, with nothing to speak for those beneath.

Vashti had attended purely for personal reasons. Purely because during her months of dealing with the old man she had come to like and respect him greatly, and she'd been genuinely saddened by his death.

Emerging from her car after a horrendous drive through drizzle and fog all the way from Hobart, she had almost got right back in again and left, thinking how out of place she felt, and probably looked, to all those gathered round the tiny church, which was literally propped up by timbers on each side and seemed almost to cower beneath the huge old pine trees surrounding the cemetery.

She was only twenty kilometres from Ouse, barely a hundred from Hobart, but it seemed as if she'd gone back just as far in time.

These were country people. Work-roughened hands tugged at unfamiliar and strangling ties and collars beneath out-of-fashion pin-striped suits. Those who were hatless had pale foreheads above tanned and weathered faces. Most of the women, too, seemed from a different time, their clothing somehow dated, their very attitudes different. Given the unique setting of the place, Vashti wouldn't have been surprised to see Model-T Fords parked around the yard, but what she did see still held a country flavour of battered utilities and four-wheel-drives parked along the narrow dirt track to the churchyard with luxury vehicles that had seen better days.

Around her as she hesitantly sought out a glimpse of the family were the voices of rural Tasmania; the talk was of cattle and rain and sheep and drought and crops. And the very cadence of those voices was audibly different, so reminiscent of old Bede Keene's way of speaking that it brought a lump to her throat.

And as more people gathered—surely the little church couldn't hold them all?—she noticed that she wasn't totally alone in not fitting in. There were a few people in city gear, a few men who stood out from the crowd because of their noticeable veneer of sophistication.

Two, she noticed, were politicians, one of them a cabinet minister for the state of Tasmania. And of course Janice Gentry, the family's accountant, was there, classically clothed, classically beautiful, but, to Vashti's eye, with an expression that said this was a duty appearance, even if the accountant seemed comfortable enough in the rural setting.

Her expression had changed as the two women met, nodded, and then Ms Gentry was past and Vashti found herself face to face with Bevan Keene, the elder of the sons, and Alana, the surprisingly young twenty-two-year-old daughter of the patriarch, who'd died in his seventy-ninth year.

Their welcome was evident; Bevan smiled at her, murmuring her name as he nodded. Alana went so far as to reach out and take Vashti's hands in a warm greeting.

Vashti had to blink back tears and force a smile of her own that froze as Alana moved aside to introduce 'my brother Phelan' and Vashti looked up to meet grey-green eyes that fairly blazed with hostility.

No words. She, transfixed by his attitude, simply couldn't speak; he clearly wasn't about to.

Instead, he stared down at her, eyes fierce, mouth fixed in a bitter, angry slash. His pale eyes seemed to burn from a darkly suntanned face the colour of his crisply curled hair. It was a wolf's face; merciless and bleak.

Vashti was stunned. Never in her life had she seen such blatant bitterness. And for what? She'd never met him before—and certainly wouldn't have forgotten if she had.

Far from handsome, at least in any conventional way, he was the most intensely *alive* man she'd ever seen. Although he was standing still, it seemed as if he was poised, totally ready for action. His immobility shouted its own lie. And, she noticed quite irrelevantly, he too was in the country yet not quite *of* it. His dark suit was of European styling, his gleaming shoes a world apart from the dress boots worn by most other men present.

His haircut was of the city, his hands work-muscled, but more the hands of an artist than a farmer. Which, of course, he wasn't. Phelan Keene was a writer and a famous one, a man who'd kept his rural background in his fitness and carriage, but whose life now was centred round the international scene, travelling in Europe and especially in south-east Asia.

And he did not like her, to say the very least. But why?

She tried to match his stare, but found it almost impossible. Had it been a frank sexual appraisal she could have managed; she'd faced enough of them in

her adult years to recognise such. But this was a predator's appraisal, so savage that she half expected to
see him snarl, to see gleaming teeth slashing down at
her trembling throat.

For what seemed like hours she felt as if there were
only the two of them there, as if they were trapped
in stillness within the quiet, sober bustle of the funeral crowd. Then he shouldered past her and it was
as if she'd been suddenly returned to a strangely men-
acing present.

Moments later, the crowd began to take on a semblance of order as everyone moved to first fill, then
overfill, the tiny church. Vashti, still shaken by Phelan
Keene's silent assault, hung back, and stayed with the
overflow outside.

The funeral, quietly dignified and somehow fitted
to the setting, finally over, she found herself in the
muddle of departing vehicles without seeing Phelan
Keene again, and wasn't sorry. Finally, she managed
to trail other vehicles southwards to Ouse, but didn't
pause for the 'wake' at the Lachlan Hotel, despite
overhearing compliments about the food and drink
that would be on offer.

Instead, she had continued on to Hobart, wondering as she drove why Phelan Keene had seemed so
angry, so hostile. It was, she had thought with no sense
of understanding, as if he somehow blamed Vashti
herself for his father's death.

All of which, she now thought, made his request
all the more surprising, not to mention suspicious.
Fair enough for him to write a book which might involve taxation office procedures, but why specifically
seek *her* involvement?

'I'll do what I can, then,' Vashti assured her boss, but she kept her fingers crossed behind her back as she did so; there was something going on here that she somehow knew she wasn't going to like.

On her way home from work, Vashti bought a paperback copy of Phelan Keene's latest suspense thriller.

The reading of it occupied the next three evenings, but did nothing to reveal the logic of the remembered antipathy towards her. Even Keene's picture on the back cover held more mystery than information; it was unsatisfyingly flat and lifeless compared to her memory of the man himself.

The picture simply couldn't do justice to those eyes, she found herself thinking. Those icy grey-green eyes, so bleak in their hostility towards her, now seemed to mock her with their blandness in the picture.

Worse, the image of Phelan Keene revealed a surprising resemblance to the man's father; Vashti might have been looking at Bede Keene in his mid-thirties, she thought.

There was the same high-bridged nose, the same generous mouth and solid, determined jawline. It was easy to picture the old man's shock of still curly grey hair as auburn and even curlier. The photograph held none of the anger she remembered from her brief meeting with the man; indeed he looked almost friendly, with one quirked eyebrow and a hint of a wry smile for his readers.

A face with character, she found herself thinking. A lived-in face. A face too much like his father's for Vashti's taste. She had liked and greatly admired the father, a man of black and white principles, a man with little compromise, and no deviousness, no great

subtleties except in the droll, dry sense of humour
she'd come to relish.

Throughout their involvement, he'd established a
joking pattern of trying to marry her off to one or
the other of his sons, insisting she was getting 'long
in the tooth' and overdue for marriage. The subject
had first arisen when he'd spoken of the original
family home north of Ouse. Now it was of only mar-
ginal significance to the family's vast empire, but it
had been the beginning, and held great emotional significance to the old man.

He'd grown up there, married there, buried his wife
there, and was far from joking when he told Vashti
he'd 'get a measure of satisfaction out of dying in the
same house I was born in. Not that it's really the same
house—probably more new than old about it now—
but still . . .'

'I can't imagine much satisfaction in dying anywhere,' she'd replied, adding, 'but then I've only got
my poky little flat, and it's rented in any case.'

'And you're far too young to be thinking of dying
anyway,' he'd said. 'You should be thinking of
children and a home of your own. *I* should be thinking
about grandchildren, by rights, but the way my mob's
going I suspect I'll not see grandchildren in the house
where I was born.'

He'd chuckled, eyes bright with inner laughter.
'Unless I could interest you in a fine, strapping lad
like Bevan, of course. Might be handy having a tax
expert in the family. Phelan,' he grunted, 'wouldn't
be much use to you; he's never here at the best of
times.'

Vashti had missed most of a muttered remark about
the second son, but the look in the old man's eyes

fairly shouted that although Phelan Keene might be wild and unruly, with little of the old man's steadiness, he was none the less a favourite.

'You'll outlive all of us,' she'd retorted, and now recalled the comment with sadness as she thought of him on that lonely ridge with generations of Bannisters and various members of the Harrex and Barry families, the many children from so long ago that were buried there with him, yet no grandchild of his own left to mourn.

A grand old man, a man worth the knowing.

But this son? She didn't know—couldn't know—could only speculate at the man behind the confusing dichotomy of picture and meeting. Phelan Keene clearly hadn't liked her, but his father *had*; of that she was certain.

When she'd finished the first novel, she searched out two others in a second-hand bookshop, and had read one of them as well by the time she finally heard from the man himself. Neither book did anything to ease her apprehensions; even less did they prepare her for the sheer seductiveness of his voice over the telephone.

'Phelan Keene,' he announced in tones that were pure chocolate fudge. 'I understand you've been designated to assist with this book I'm trying to work up.'

'I've agreed to help where I can,' Vashti replied, not exactly being evasive, but hoping at the same time to avoid sounding too eager.

It was difficult; Phelan Keene's voice fairly rippled with sex appeal, touching her as surely as if he had been there in the room, stroking, caressing, exploring.

'We'll have to get together in person, soon,' he was suggesting, and that voice did more than simply suggest. 'I was hoping to at least have lunch together before we got into the details of my research, but I seem to have got ahead of my own schedule for once, and already I have questions that are slowing me up.'

'We couldn't have that, could we?' Vashti replied without thinking, then could have bitten her tongue. What a thing to say!

Phelan Keene seemed not to notice. He began, instead, to work through what was obviously a list of questions he had already prepared. Most of them, Vashti was comforted to find, seemed direct enough and easy to answer.

But then she began to detect a pattern, or at least the beginnings of a pattern. And it was a pattern that did nothing at all for her peace of mind, harking back, as it now clearly did, to her work with Phelan Keene's father and family, to the field audit and the philosophy behind it.

Vashti shook her head, both alarmed and worried by the direction the conversation was taking. There was, she now knew, absolutely nothing drastic hidden among the myriad accounts administered—in theory— by Janice Gentry; indeed, the family business was almost certain to emerge from the field audit with flying colours. But something about the way Phelan Keene now approached the subject was a red danger signal to Vashti.

'Really, Mr Keene,' she finally had to say, 'I think this is getting far off the track of being just research. It seems you're getting on to fairly specific ground here, and I'm not sure we ought to be discussing such details.'

'Why not? Have you got something to hide?'

'Certainly not, but policy prohibits me from discussing specific cases, which it seems to me you're leading up to.'

'It's a case in which I'm personally involved. It isn't as if I were asking you to discuss somebody else's business.' His voice was still so smooth, so persuasive.

'I realise that,' Vashti replied, 'but again, Mr Keene, I have to say that I'm not comfortable about discussing this specific case outside a formal situation with your family's accountant in attendance. I don't ... don't think we should go on with this at this time.'

'Too right you don't ... *Ms* Sinclair.' Despite the rich, mellow sound of his voice, he managed to make the honorific 'Ms' sound somehow tawdry, or at the very least pretentious.

Vashti's temper flared, then was as quickly brought under control before she could snap a reply into the telephone. She suddenly guessed—and just in time— what he was on about and why the entire conversation had suddenly taken on a tinge of *déjà vu*.

Gotcha! she thought, and almost laughed aloud. The very nerve of the illustrious Mr Keene! He was playing games with her, had been all along.

'Could you hold for just a tick?' she asked, and, without waiting for an answer, she put down the telephone and turned to quickly rush across the room and grab her handbag.

Returning to her desk, it was the work of a moment to grab up the copy of the book she'd only just started reading and find the passage she wanted.

Forcing the book down hard in front of her, Vashti skimmed through the pages and fought to steady her breathing and still summon the courage for what she was about to try.

'You seem to have something against the use of the word "Ms", *Mr* Keene.' Vashti deliberately kept her voice rigidly calm, undramatic. It wouldn't do to give the game away by her tone of voice alone. 'I wouldn't have expected a man in your position to be such a blatant chauvinist.'

'Chauvinism has nothing to do with it. I just don't like having to refer to any woman by a word that's at best wishy-washy and at worst nothing more than an abbreviation for manuscript,' he snapped in reply, and Vashti could have cried out with delight.

He was following the script! Just as if he, also, had the book there in front of him; as if he, too, could read the hero's lines that *he* had written.

Vashti grinned to herself, silently wondering how far she could carry the performance. She forgot, for the moment, that she was working, and plunged into the game with a vengeance.

'A manuscript? Is that really the way you see me?' she purred, lost in a mental picture of the book's scenario as Phelan Keene had created it.

'Be an interesting concept—if I were blind—for both of us,' he replied, and now that rich chocolate-brown voice was softer, sliding into a resonance that was dangerously seductive.

Vashti, reading as he spoke, found herself mentally picturing Phelan Keene himself as the hero of the piece. And, strangely—almost dreamily—herself as the heroine. It wasn't all that difficult; the girl in the book was also short, with long ash-blonde hair, and wore glasses. Her figure...well, Vashti had never considered herself quite so voluptuous, but by the same token she was quite happy with her body. She did, she knew, have very good legs—at least as good as Keene's heroine.

'Braille? I'd ... hate to think my skin was all *that* rough,' she replied, reading and yet not reading; acting.

'So would I.'

His voice was husky now, as he reached out to take her wrist in his fingers, fingers that brushed the thin skin of her inner wrist with the delicacy of a kiss ...

She pulled away, suddenly fearful, her heart hammering. This man could too easily take control of this situation, she realised, could too easily take control of *her*! ...

'The masculine honorific, after all, doesn't concern itself with whether a man's married or not,' Vashti said.

But even free, she could feel his touch like a burn on her wrist, could feel the tingle all the way through her body. She thought she was trembling, tried not to ...

'Perhaps because it doesn't matter?'

His voice was still soft, his eyes now close—too close. She could see the tiny dark rays that ran through the startling blue, could actually see the desire in ...

'Fair is fair,' she replied. 'If *Mr* doesn't tell me whether *you're* married or not, then I can't see why a woman should be forced to——'

'Forced?'

Now it was his eyes that touched her, and if anything that was worse. Because his eyes didn't stop at her wrist; his eyes touched all of her, brushed firmness into her nipples, crept enticingly along the flat plane of her stomach...

'Who said anything about force, *Ms* Sinclair?'

The pages of the book blurred before Vashti's eyes; she momentarily lost her place and found herself gasping for a quick breath, a shake of her head that left her wide-eyed at the strangeness she felt.

'You...you...' she faltered.

'...wrote the book!' he snapped, now departed from the script, no longer the heroic, fictional character in a book, now a too real voice on the telephone that threatened to drop from Vashti's suddenly nerveless fingers.

No chocolate fudge in the voice now. It snapped across the phone wires like a lash, flaying both her ear and her conscience.

'Credit for trying, *Ms* Sinclair. Inventive, to say the very least. But you should have *finished* the book before you started playing silly little games. You might have found out that she *didn't* win in the end, didn't get the hero in the end.'

The sound of him hanging up was like·a physical blow; there was a dreadful sense of finality to it that was curiously mingled with foreboding.

Vashti sat there, staring sightlessly at Phelan Keene's book on the desk before her, the telephone receiver now humming. The book had flapped shut and his picture stared up at her accusingly, the half-smile caught by the photographer suddenly not a smile at all, but the beginnings of a predatory grin.

CHAPTER TWO

THE second time Vashti spoke with Phelan Keene started as another unmitigated disaster, improved not at all by the fact that Vashti knew it was all her own fault.

She was sitting in Janice Gentry's office when he arrived, along with his brother and sister, and had they come without Phelan she actually might have been quite glad to see them.

Being ten minutes early—Vashti had often considered her habits of punctuality to be a curse—had forced her into a lengthy session of supposedly polite chatter with the accountant. Polite on the surface, at least. Vashti hadn't liked Janice Gentry when they'd been at university together, and had since found little to change her mind about the woman.

Not that she would ever—during her time at university—have expected Janice Gentry even to know she existed. They had moved in vastly different social circles, to put it mildly.

Janice Gentry was 'old' money in Tasmanian terms. Her family had been among the island state's so-called 'squattocracy', descendants of early land-grant settlers at a time when, historically, most of the island's population was drawn from convicts or former convicts. Her family had left the land and formed a dynasty in Hobart business circles before Janice came on the scene, Vashti knew, but the dark-haired ac-

19

countant's claim to social acceptance was solid enough.

While Vashti had worked her way through university with the help of a scholarship, Janice Gentry had used her father's money and social position to the utmost. No academic slouch by any standard, she had gained her degree by working only *just* hard enough; studies came a poor second place to the social opportunities.

She had moved into her father's firm, as expected, and then, also as expected, had gravitated to head the firm at his poor-health-forced retirement only a year before. But, even before Janice took over, the firm had been less than popular with the taxation office; her ascendancy to the top had improved nothing.

And if she hadn't noticed Vashti during their days at university, it was clear she wasn't about to start now. They had spent the ten minutes on reminiscences so startlingly different, they mightn't have been at the same university.

The enforced falseness of this polite time-wasting had done little for Vashti's already fragile mood. This would be, she hoped, the final official meeting required to tidy up all the loose ends in the field audit, but she had been dreading the meeting just on the presumption that Phelan Keene might attend; when he walked into the office she could only rise to her feet politely and hope her nerveless legs would support her.

Suddenly she knew, without even knowing why she knew, that it *wouldn't* be the final meeting, that somehow Phelan Keene was going to complicate things. And that the complications would have nothing at all to do with the book he was supposedly researching.

Bevan and Alana greeted her with their usual friendliness, Alana especially effusive in her greeting. Vashti had liked the 'baby' of the family from their very first meeting, and although both girls claimed compatibility because of their size—Alana was an inch shorter even than Vashti—it really went beyond that.

'You don't look all that well, if you don't mind me saying so,' Alana said with concern as she reached out to take both of Vashti's hands in her own. 'Have you got the dreaded lurg that's been going round?'

Vashti didn't dare look at Phelan Keene, who stood behind his brother and sister. How would he, she wondered, react to hearing himself described as a contagious disease?

'I'm fine,' she assured the diminutive Alana. 'I've just had a few . . . late nights lately.' She dared to look up then, only to realise she'd put her foot in it again!

Phelan's pale eyes fairly danced with satisfaction as he murmured, 'With a good book?' then gave a fierce bark of laughter as Vashti flushed with embarrassment.

The soft query brought questioning glances from his brother and sister, but Phelan ignored them, striding over to sit at the side of the room, where he fixed Vashti with his pale eyes and proceeded to thoroughly demoralise her.

He'd chosen his position, she realised immediately, just so that he could deliberately stir. The angle of his position let him watch Vashti's every move and, worse, force her attention to be diverted at his choosing, without the others catching him at it.

They were concentrating mostly on what Janice Gentry was saying, and on Vashti's responses. Vashti found herself attacked on both flanks, and unable to defend either one adequately as a result.

This is a farce, she told herself, having had to ask the same question for the third time as Phelan's scrutiny and faint sneer destroyed her concentration. Most of the discussion involved going over old ground, but even that familiarity couldn't help her forever.

'There just isn't the documentation,' she found herself saying, again repeating herself. Oh, damn... damn... damn, she thought, increasingly annoyed at how easily Phelan Keene could get her goat, and knowing it was all because she'd let herself be drawn into playing silly games on the telephone.

The worst of it was that Phelan hardly said a word. He let Janice Gentry and his brother Bevan carry the arguments, with no more than the occasional slightly cocked eyebrow, usually at Vashti's responses.

But he didn't really have to speak to be effective. He managed that only too well, just with his eyes and his overall body language.

If Vashti dared glance his way, it was to find those *knowing*, icy grey-green eyes undressing her, peeling away her clothing as distinctly as if he could physically touch her, could actually undo the buttons of her sensible office blouse, could feel for himself the whimsical lace of her bra, the soft swelling of her breasts.

Certainly *she* could feel the physical manifestation of his mental assault. Beneath the bra her nipples throbbed, as sensitive to her thoughts as to his touch.

She had to consciously restrain herself from shifting in her chair, her thighs warm beneath her tights.

Damn him anyway, she thought, mentally squirming, because she couldn't do so physically. Bad enough he was able to manipulate her so—but the rotter was so obviously enjoying it!

By the meeting's end, she had conceded several points, mostly because she had intended to in any event. Even with sketchy documentation, old Bede Keene's intentions were clear enough, and there was no evidence even to *suggest* tax evasion on his part.

One major issue still remained, however, the ultimate interpretation of which could have significant effects throughout the wool-growing sector. It was this which had sparked the field audit in the first place, only to be submerged in the welter of partially related affairs linked to old Bede Keene's personal dealings. One more meeting, at least, Vashti realised, would be required to finally sort that one out, since Bevan Keene said he thought there might be a bit more documentation available.

'I'm sure I saw it when we were sorting things out at the farm,' he said, for the first time drawing Phelan into the discussion.

'More than possible; I'm still finding things I didn't know existed,' was the reply. 'The old man got to be even more of a pack-rat as he got older. I'm surprised we're having any trouble at all finding written evidence of his dealings; he kept everything else.'

'Phelan's staying on at the farm for now,' his brother explained to Vashti, who already knew Bevan and Alana lived on separate family properties—he in the northern Midlands and she on a smaller, intensively cropped property served by the new irrigation scheme centred below the Colebrook reservoir.

'We're off to lunch, Vashti. Why don't you join us?' asked Alana with her usual spontaneity. The invitation, to Vashti's great surprise, caused a noticeable flicker of annoyance to cross Janice Gentry's face.

Vashti's immediate reaction was an overwhelming no. Not just that it was rather against policy, not even that she'd had more than enough already of Janice Gentry... It was the look she caught from Phelan Keene.

But before she had a chance to say anything, *he* did.

'It isn't that I want to be antisocial,' he said. 'And I'm sure Ms Sinclair doesn't either. But we have further business to discuss, she and I, so if it's all right with you lot we'll be having lunch... together but without you.'

'I——' She got no further.

'You don't believe in lunching with *clients*, I suppose,' he interjected. 'But it is lunchtime and you do have to eat, same as the rest of us, and we *do* have a few things to discuss, do we not?'

'Yes... but...'

'Yes... but what? If you're worried about being compromised I suggest you think again. I don't compromise pretty girls in public, and I'm off back to the bush right after, so stop being all public service and *thing*, and come along. We'll go over the road, I think.'

He had taken her arm and was leading her from the office before Vashti could properly object, waving a farewell to the others and saying at the same time, 'I *did* mention on the phone that I'd hoped to have lunch with you; there's no need to seem quite so surprised.'

Vashti said nothing. She found herself struck mute, as if his fingers above her elbow had cut off some vital nerve to her tongue. They walked to the lift together, descended to street level, and emerged into Hobart's city centre without her saying a single word.

Phelan Keene didn't even appear to notice. He chatted on about something—she might have been deaf as well because it just didn't get into her ears—holding her arm in the meanwhile as if they were the best of friends or...or more.

And suddenly it was too much—too much and far too fast. Twisting free, Vashti gabbled out the first excuse that came to mind—anything to keep herself free of his touch.

'I...I've just remembered I have to get to the bank,' she stammered. 'In case I don't have time after work.' The light had changed, but Vashti was no longer paying attention. Half her mind was on walking back towards the Trust Bank of Tasmania building; all of her instincts were crying out to her to just run...run anywhere that would get her away from Phelan Keene.

Phelan Keene—who didn't appear to notice her confusion—was oblivious to her panic. 'OK,' he said. 'But don't be too long about it; I'm more than just a bit peckish.'

Vashti nodded her assurance, meanwhile reaching into her handbag for her wallet and the card that would activate the automatic cash machine.

Phelan stood back courteously as she fed the card into the machine, punched in the complicated series of identification numbers, and collected the notes that eventually emerged.

She stuffed the money into her wallet and turned to find him standing there, shaking his head and frowning slightly. 'You really ought to be ashamed of yourself,' he said.

'Why, for goodness' sake?' Vashti genuinely had no idea what he was on about, and wasn't, it appeared, to be told just yet, either.

'Later, maybe,' he muttered, shaking his head. 'It might just be me; I tend to get cranky on an empty stomach.'

They crossed the street and turned up Murray Street to an historic hotel, where Vashti was somehow unsurprised to find Phelan greeted by name when they entered, and they were courteously shown to a quiet corner table in the restaurant. She so seldom dined out that she'd be lucky to recognise a restaurant's name, much less have staff remember hers, Vashti thought, then shrugged the thought away as unworthy.

Phelan, she thought, looked perfectly at home here. He was dressed in the type of semi-casual clothes preferred by country folk in Tasmania—a Harris Tweed sports jacket, moleskin trousers and elastic-sided boots. And now that he wasn't glaring furiously at her, as he had during the funeral, he looked more the man on the cover of his books.

The crisp, curly dark brown hair was well cut and tidy enough, except when he thrust his fingers through it in absent thought. His grin was almost infectious, if rare. Only the eyes hadn't changed. Against the depth of his tan they were astonishingly pale, difficult to read.

They ordered, Vashti refusing a drink on the legitimate grounds that 'I wouldn't get any work at all done this afternoon; a big lunch will be quite enough of a shock to the system, thank you.'

'I can't imagine your system being that easily shocked,' was the response. 'But then again...' He let the comment drag out, stretching it much as he had persisted in stretching out the 'Mssss' whenever he addressed her.

'It's a very simple system, I assure you,' she replied, almost calm now, almost composed, despite knowing he could upset her composure almost at will.

Vashti sipped at her tomato juice when it arrived, too aware of his eyes upon her, of how he seemed to be ever watchful, attuned to her every movement and thought.

His telephone accusation, not once mentioned during the meeting or—yet—now that they were alone together, still grated. How dared he accuse her like that? she thought. And immediately felt her anger begin to push away her spate of nerves.

She took a deep breath, as subtly as she could manage it, then put down the glass and reached up to adjust her glasses as she looked at him squarely.

'Now, Mr Keene,' she said firmly, 'perhaps we can begin?'

'Do that again,' he replied, and she saw his eyes gleam with what seemed to be laughter.

'Do what again?' she countered, immediately cautious. What on earth was he on about this time?'

Now he grinned, and reached out to shove imaginary glasses into place on his nose. 'Makes you look all fierce and authoritarian, like an...a... schoolteacher.'

'What kind of schoolteacher?' She hadn't missed the hesitation, could have inserted 'old maid' easily enough herself, but suddenly wanted to see if she could push him into admitting it.

'A rather pretty one, actually,' he replied, his grin broadening but his eyes somehow making the comment far more intimate than it sounded.

Vashti shook her head, but said nothing. It was too dangerous to play word games with this man, she told herself, but couldn't help it.

Neither could she help the habitual gesture of adjusting her glasses, and, without realising it until too late, she did it again! And Phelan Keene, of course, nodded his approval with a quirky grin. She could have kicked herself.

'I suppose you're bound and determined this is to be all business,' he said then with an exaggerated sigh. 'Can't we at least wait until we've had the starter? I'm absolutely famished and, as I told you, I get fair-dinkum cranky when I'm hungry.'

And *I* get fair-dinkum cranky when I'm being stuffed around, she wanted to say, but didn't. She didn't say a word, in fact, just nodded agreement at the first part of his statement.

He frowned at her determination, but the frown changed to a wide grin of satisfaction as their starter arrived. 'Saved by the bell,' he chuckled, thanking the waitress, who—Vashti couldn't help noticing—was wondrously appreciative of every morsel of attention Phelan Keene deigned to proffer.

Style, she found herself admitting. And what's worse, he does it without even having to think about it. The man's a born womaniser; he flirts and flatters and *manipulates* just for the hell of it. So watch yourself!

Which she did, concentrating on her scallops, while being only too aware that *he* was concentrating more on her than on the scrumptious-looking Barilla Bay oysters he appeared to so enjoy.

But it was all too brief a respite. Vashti nibbled at the last tasty morsel and wished she'd claimed to be on a diet or something, so that this would be the end of the meal and she could then plead some excuse to return to work. And then asked herself why, because sooner or later she would have to deal with Phelan Keene and his damned book! Maybe the sooner the better, she thought; at least it'll be over and done with.

But it wasn't. While they waited for their main courses, Phelan showed no sign of wanting to get down to business. He commented on the quality of the food, solicitously enquired whether Vashti wouldn't reconsider and have wine with her duckling, but gave her no opportunity to force the conversation back on to purely business footings.

Nor was she as ready as before to force the issue. Now her instincts told her to be totally cautious, to volunteer nothing, expect only the unexpected. I'm being set up, she thought, but I don't know for what, much less why.

Thankfully, she was able to devote her full attention to the delicious roast duckling when it arrived, impatiently putting aside a mild feeling of envy when she looked over at the thick rib of beef he was consuming with obvious pleasure.

I'd feel the same way if *he* were having the duckling and I the steak, she realised; the issue wasn't the dish on offer but the fact that Phelan Keene had taken the privilege of ordering for her.

'You needn't look so envious,' he said with a wry grin. 'All that talk about having to work this afternoon, I reckoned a steak this size would have you dozing in your chair by smoko.'

Vashti nearly choked. What was it with this man? Surely he couldn't be reading her mind? Then she sobered and glared at him across the table. Observant, that was all. Logical for a writer, she supposed, but unnerving for all that.

She thought for an instant of asking him if he made a habit of verbalising his observations, then thought better of it; he'd probably only say what she'd been thinking, and she didn't feel up to any cryptic references to writing or—worse—books just for now.

'I'm a bit surprised at you,' he said after a moment. 'Either you hide your feminine curiosity rather well, or...'

'Or what?'

'Or I'm losing my touch,' he admitted bluntly. 'I would have expected some sort of question by now about my comment at the bank, although I realise you've been trying hard to keep our relationship totally businesslike.'

'Should it be anything else?' she replied calmly. Phelan Keene might need food to keep from being cranky, but Vashti had just discovered how much a good meal improved her whole mental outlook. For the first time that day, she actually felt totally capable of dealing with his attempts to stir her up.

'But OK, I'll play your litle game.' She shrugged. 'What did I do at the bank that so got on your wick? Wasn't I secretive enough while I was punching numbers into that stupid automatic cash machine or something? If I was, it's hardly anything surprising.

I hate the damned things with a veritable passion, but, the hours I keep, there aren't many alternatives.'

Phelan grinned. 'The issue wasn't secrecy—just plain old inconsideration,' he reflected. 'Although I suppose you didn't notice that there were six healthy, hale and hearty *human* bank clerks standing round that bank twiddling their little thumbs while you were standing out on the street in a line of people talking to a damned machine! It's worse than just inconsiderate—it's downright insulting!'

His voice rose gradually throughout the diatribe, to the point where one or two people at adjacent tables actually looked up. Vashti sat there with her mouth open, absolutely stunned.

All she could do was look at him, wide-eyed, a fork full of food halfway to her mouth, and—in her mind—gasp like a stranded fish. Phelan Keene, meanwhile, sat glaring at her as if she'd kicked his dog. They sat there for what seemed hours, silently looking at each other.

'Sorry about that,' he finally said, voice thankfully lower now, although without a sign of real remorse. 'One of my hobby-horses, obviously, and I *did* warn you that hunger makes me cranky.'

'It's a bit late for that excuse,' Vashti replied with a meaningful glance at his nearly empty plate. 'And don't you dare blame it on the wine, either; that's Piper's Brook, and I'm sure you know how good it is, considering you're paying for it.'

'And will end up taking most of it home with me,' he snapped crossly. 'You can see I've only had two glasses, and I'm damned if I'll lay myself open to a drink-driving charge.'

'I should certainly hope not. And don't change the subject,' she replied just as snappily, delighted at actually having *him* on the back foot for a change. 'Don't you think it's just a bit much to invite me to lunch—to coerce me into having lunch with you, not to put too fine a point on it—and then start criticising my banking habits, of all things?'

'I brought it up before lunch, actually,' he replied without the slightest sign of contrition. 'And, I might add, without so much as mentioning the fact that if you were going to use a machine that's available twenty-four hours a day there was hardly the panic involved you tried to portray. You could have got your money any time.'

'I don't care *when* you brought it up,' Vashti hissed. 'I think you've got a nerve bringing it up at all! It is none of your business. None!'

Vashti was working herself up into a frothing good rage, however artificial, when the waitress arrived to clear away their dinner plates. It was quite obvious that the woman was only too aware of the hostile atmosphere between them, but to Vashti's astonishment the waitress looked at *her* as if she were the sole cause of the argument. Phelan Keene got just what Vashti would have expected—a look which clearly took his side entirely in the matter.

And from the look on Phelan's face, he and waitress agreed!

That was enough to make her truly wild. Vashti found herself clenching and unclenching her fists beneath the table, her fingernails biting into her palms. Her breath came in short, sharp huffs, and it seemed as if the entire room were closing in around her, the very air electric with her anger.

She was conscious, as the waitress turned away, of actually holding her breath, waiting for the woman to get just far enough before she let fly.

'This, I think, is the moment where you're supposed to throw something at me, grab up your handbag, and stomp out in high dudgeon, whatever that is.' His voice was low, but with those rich chocolate-brown tones it carried across the table like a shout. Or a challenge.

'In some pulp fiction epics, written by people who shall remain nameless, and present company definitely *not* excepted.' Vashti spat out the words, her voice even more controlled than his. 'But this isn't fiction, *Mr* Keene; this is the real world. This is Hobart, Tasmania, and I'm a real person. I'm not so sure about you.'

Vashti pushed up her glasses, instantly regretted the gesture, but *only* for an instant, then returned to the attack.

'So how about *you* throw something and stomp off in high dudgeon? Presuming you can spell it. Try throwing money to pay for this... this...' She sputtered, but not to a stop. 'Because *I'm* going to have the biggest, richest dessert on the menu, and I'd like to be able to enjoy it without being hassled about my... my banking habits!'

She was half out of her chair now, one lacquered fingernail aimed like a gun between those fathomless grey-green eyes, her own eyes blazing and her words hanging almost visibly above the table.

Phelan sat immobile, his long, craftsman's fingers splayed on the table before him. His jaw was clenched, and she could see the muscles flexing, as if he was gnashing his teeth in a fury that matched her own.

But when he finally spoke, it was in a voice of such soft, reasoned calm that she surprisedly became aware of her posture, and quite suddenly sat back down.

'You're right, of course. And I do apologise—honestly.' He threw open his hands in a gesture that would have been provocatively flamboyant except that his eyes told her the truth. Under her glare, he paused, then continued, and this time his words confirmed it.

'You said earlier you don't go much on those damnable automatic cash machines,' he said, steepling his fingers before him on the table. 'Well, I positively *hate* the things, although I have to admit my feelings aren't wholly altruistic. True, it really gets my dander up when I go into a bank and find half a dozen clerks standing around doing nothing while people line up outside to use machines. I think it's a tragic sign of the times that so many people would rather deal with a machine instead of a *person*.'

'When you work the hours I do, there often isn't all that much notice,' Vashti interrupted, only to have him shush her with one upraised finger, then at least have the grace to look slightly embarrassed when she obeyed.

'After hours isn't the issue,' he said, eyes now blazing with what Vashti thought a writer would call impassioned fervour. 'It's during the day that I'm talking about—during normal business hours, when bank clerks are being paid to be there, to be of service, to do their jobs, for goodness' sake. And nobody will let them. They have to stand there with fixed little smiles on their faces and watch—*watch*, mind you!—while people ignore them in favour of *machines*! How the hell can anybody get job satisfaction out of that?'

Vashti shook her head, uncertain what, if anything, to say, not certain, indeed, if she was to be given a chance, until the waitress arrived with the sweets menu and she was able to echo Phelan's earlier remark.

'Saved by the bell . . . again?'

His grin was infectious.

'Too right. And please, without any arguments, may I be permitted to order this wondrous dessert you're going to have? It's a small price for my sins.'

'I'd reckon! *Your* sins, I suspect, would have a far, far higher price than that,' Vashti retorted. But her grin matched his; she simply couldn't help herself.

'A deal, then? No names, no pack drill?'

'Deal,' she replied, but hesitated momentarily before reaching out to meet the hand he extended across the table. Their eyes met with, she thought, some unknown-as-yet message as his fingers closed around her own, and he held her hand just sufficiently too long, or was it not long enough?

She was saved the problem of deciding with the return of the waitress, and Phelan's grandiose announcement that he wanted the biggest, richest, most awe-inspiring dessert on the sweets menu.

'And my mother'll have the same,' he said, flashing Vashti the most mischievous, devilish little-boy grin she'd ever seen.

The waitress smiled; Vashti thought the woman would have smiled no matter what Phelan said. Chauvinistic bastard! Vashti bit her tongue but didn't smile. Instead she shot Phelan a look of warning, in the certain knowledge that it was wasted.

'You really do like living dangerously, don't you?' she muttered when the woman was truly out of earshot. 'What is it—a death-wish? Or do you just like to stir?'

'I sometimes wonder myself,' he replied, leaning calmly back in his chair, as if the knives she was glaring at him couldn't possibly get across the table. 'You do stir awfully easily, I must say. I'd have thought a decent sense of humour would be vital in your job.'

'And I'd have thought just *some* sense would be vital in yours,' Vashti retorted. 'Do you live your whole life in some fictional wonderland where you can just write your way out of trouble? I am the dreaded taxman, in case you've forgotten.'

She put on her sternest face as she said it, the face she used when the powers of her office were needed in full to bring some really difficult client into line. It was needed seldom, but when it was...

Stern look or no, it was supposed to be funny, supposed to match the mood Phelan Keene had created. But it wasn't, suddenly. Something... something she couldn't quite identify... came to life in his eyes, and Vashti instantly cursed herself for such an unprofessional gambit.

You fool, she cried inwardly. Fool... fool... fool! She recognised the predator, the wolf that had so fleetingly stalked out to glare at her. She'd seen that look before, in a lonely cemetery where she'd been the subject of a longer, more thorough inspection.

And just as quickly, the predator was gone. Phelan's eyes now were bland, placid. She'd seen that colour— exactly—in the water over shallow reefs, and once in the wild eyes of a blue merle collie just before it tried to lunch on her left leg.

Vashti shivered inwardly, still cursing herself for her transgression. She wanted to take it back, to say something—anything—but the chance had disappeared as quickly as that fleeting predator's glance.

'Yes, I suppose I should remember that, shouldn't I?'

Phelan's expression was as bland as his eyes now, too bland. 'Especially as we never did get to the real purpose of this luncheon, which was supposed to be business,' he continued, voice calm, strangely flat.

'Still,' he said with a grin that never reached his eyes, 'there's dessert to come.'

And come it did! The sheer size of the offerings was such that Vashti and Phelan could only stare first at their plates and then at each other, animosity forgotten—or so Vashti hoped—in the face of such gastronomic opulence.

Each of them managed half their dessert, eating in silence at first, then with timid forays into the kind of small talk that the meal had begun with. There was no business, and now Vashti was glad of that. She felt embarrassed at having come the heavy; however frivolous the move had been it had been a bad one, seriously misinterpreted.

Far easier to let Phelan relate the other reason he hated the automatic cash machines . . .

'So there I was, Friday night of a long weekend, with not a single soul whom I knew within a thousand miles and no money worth mentioning, the damned car with a flat tyre and a flatter spare—just the scenario they advertise as being the time your cash card will save you,' he said. 'And what did the automatic cash machine do?'

'It ate the card, of course,' Vashti answered. 'There's nothing surprising about that; it's hardly an uncommon occurrence. You probably didn't get the PIN number right or something.'

'I did too!'

'Well, you must have got *something* wrong,' she insisted. 'These machines don't just go around eating people's cards at random.'

'Want to bet?'

'No, I don't want to bet. What I want to know is what you did *after* the machine ate your card. It must have been a bit traumatic, to say the least.'

'Traumatic? I was fairly ropable, as you can imagine, and on the Tuesday morning I had meaningful dialogue with the bank, let me tell you.'

'And in the meantime?'

'Oh, I just checked into the best hotel in town and lived it up for the weekend.' He shrugged. 'They didn't ask for any money until I checked out, and of course, by then I had plenty.'

'Lucky for you.' Vashti didn't even attempt to sound sympathetic. She hardly knew anybody who hadn't faced similar problems with the technology. 'And I suppose you've never used a cash card after hours *since*, either?'

'Now you're being sarcastic,' was the reply. 'Of course I have; that's what they're for. But I also——' with a hint of smugness '—make sure I'm never caught quite that short of real, usable money. It meant I had to eat every meal in the hotel's restaurant, and while it wasn't bad or anything, it got a bit boring by the end.'

'Not as boring as going hungry would have been. Or having to sleep in the streets.'

'But the card, or lack of it, had nothing to do with that,' he protested. 'I could have stayed in the hotel and charged everything whether I'd had the damned card or not! And having the card stuck in the machine all weekend meant I *had* to stay. Even if I'd somehow managed to get the car fixed, I *had* to stay because of the machine. That's the point!'

Then he grinned, again with that light of mischief in his eyes. 'Still, I got a scenario for a book out of it, so the weekend wasn't a total waste. But that doesn't change the fact that I don't like those machines, never have and never will!'

'And you never, ever use an automatic cash machine during working hours, I know,' she concluded for him. 'And while I wouldn't want you to get big-headed about this, you've actually converted me to that philosophy as well. I'm forced to admit it never occurred to me to consider how the bank clerks must feel about it.'

'Well, there you go! A taxman...person who's human after all,' he sad. 'Will wonders never cease?'

Vashti sighed. 'I do wish you'd let up on that,' she said. 'It's old hat to me, and I'm long past being offended by comments like that. Really.'

He raised one dark eyebrow. 'Well, let's just hope the chef's not easily offended either,' he said, with a meaningful glance at their half-full dessert plates. 'Because with the best will in the world I couldn't finish this, and I don't really think a doggy-bag is appropriate, somehow.'

After the lunch, they walked together back to the corner of Collins and Murray Streets, where Vashti would turn north to return to her office.

'It doesn't appear we're going to get much business done today, either,' he said as they prepared to part. 'Not that it matters much; I'm in no screaming hurry. It might be better, all things considered, if we waited on the book stuff until the family audit is finished. What do you think?'

Vashti wasn't about to create any new misunderstandings. 'If it has to be, it has to be,' she replied. 'This business seems to have more delays than real progress sometimes.'

Phelan Keene merely laughed. 'With the amount of provisional tax I'm usually up for, any delay is a blessing in disguise,' he retorted. 'I suppose I'd be in terrible strife if I somehow managed one year to have all my records just disappear in a puff of smoke?'

'You could try,' Vashti replied with a grin. 'Remembering of course that tax law is perhaps the only area of law where you're automatically presumed guilty until proven innocent—and the proof usually has to come from you!

'Records *have* been lost, of course. But I really would have to advise you to try and avoid it, and to have a very, very good accountant or tax advisor if it did happen.'

'Ah, but of course I have,' he replied. 'The very best, and extremely attractive in the bargain. I'll be right. And thanks for joining me for lunch, by the way. Even if we didn't get any business done, it was very enjoyable.'

As Vashti headed north towards her office she found herself reflecting not on the lunch—which had indeed been enjoyable—but on Phelan's coment about his accountant.

The ravishing Janice Gentry, of course, she thought, and shrugged off a vague sense of disquiet. Of course he'd have Janice Gentry as an accountant. It was only logical, since she handled the family's affairs. And certainly she was extremely attractive, no sense in denying that.

Too attractive, she found herself thinking on several occasions during what turned out to be a cow of an afternoon. Vashti put her bad temper down to too much dessert, knowing she was fooling nobody, including herself.

CHAPTER THREE

VASHTI didn't see or hear from Phelan Keene for more than a week—at least not in the flesh. He turned up on the ABC's book programme one night in what she thought must have been an old interview, but there was nothing old about the picture of him in the Hobart *Mercury* social pages.

He was resplendently dressed in evening wear, as was his predictable companion. Janice Gentry, if the grainy black and white picture was any guide, might have been wearing an evening gown—what there was of it—in leech-green, so tightly was she attached to Phelan's arm.

Vashi told herself it was irrelevant and none of her business anyway, and used that section of the paper to wrap up her rubbish.

The radio programme was quite a different story, sneaking up on her without warning as she was wishing herself to sleep after what had been a fair bitch of a day.

Having Keene's rich voice right there, next to her ear on her very own pillow, somehow sounded different from how she remembered it. It was gentler, more mellow. And, she quickly realised, it was a highly revealing voice—too revealing!

She'd turned on the radio part-way into the programme, at a point where he was reading bits of his own work and explaining some of the background.

42

Only after a few minutes did the interview itself begin, and Vashti was immediately wide awake with interest.

'Any man who says he understands women is either a damned fool or a liar—or both!' he was saying. 'In fact there are times I don't think *women* understand women; certainly *I* don't make any claims in that direction.'

'And yet your heroines seem...well...so well rounded—as people, I mean,' cooed the interviewer, and Vashti could literally *see* Phelan pouring on the charm. The interviewer's first few questions had clearly been designed to set Phelan up for something, but without even appearing to notice, he'd turned the entire thing round to his favour.

And he continued to do it. He's playing her like a piano, Vashti said to herself, fully awake now and fascinated by the whole performance. If she hadn't personally seen and heard Phelan Keene in action, his performance on the radio mightn't have been so obvious, she thought. And then she recalled how he'd done much the same to her both in person and over the telephone.

'Well, you won't do it again, and that's for sure,' she said aloud, then wondered if the opportunity would even arise.

As the interview continued, Vashti found herself swinging between anger, laughter and downright astonishment as Phelan manipulated the poor woman asking the questions.

'You should be in politics, my lad,' she found herself muttering after one exchange in which he deftly managed to appear to answer a particularly awkward question without really answering it at all.

And when the question came, as she had already come to expect, about money and how much a *famous* writer could make, it was no surprise to find him evading that one too. The real surprise came afterwards.

'The taxation system is enough to drive any sane person quite mad,' he said. 'One of these days I think I'll write a book about it, I think. Like every other businessman in the country, I spend half my time working for them anyway; it might be useful to get something back. Of course I'd have to find the right sort for a heroine, which might be tricky.'

It drew a chuckle from the woman interviewer. 'The tax—er—*person* as a heroine?' she asked. 'I'll look forward to reading that one, Mr Keene. I wouldn't have thought it possible.'

'Anything's possible in fiction,' he replied. 'That's what makes it so wonderful—the ability to create impossibilities like honest politicians and tax systems that make sense, and actually make people believe them.'

From that point, the brief remainder of the interview returned to discussions of his books, but Vashti didn't, couldn't, listen any more. She'd read the books, even enjoyed them. Now she found herself wondering—dreading the thought—if she was going to somehow be *in* one!

The concept, she realised with actual surprise, was worse than terrifying. A very, very private person, she found the whole idea so unnerving that she hardly slept all night. Because it was just what she might expect from Phelan Keene, she realised, especially considering his apparent opinion that she might in some way be responsible for having driven his father

to his death. It was all too, too complicated. And
scary!

You cunning, devious, rotten sod, she thought,
staring past her morning coffee after a troubled night.
Through the window of her small flat she could see
cloud perched like a gay pink bonnet round the crown
of Mount Wellington, heralding a day in which it
should be safe to walk to work.

The radio confirmed it, only to become a liar when
Vashti was half a block from the office. By the time
she'd actually reached her desk and could begin work
she had run her tights trying to open an umbrella that
exploded into useless tatters, dropped an armful of
papers into a muddled heap that clogged the corridor,
and broken the back off an earring.

The entire week seemed to get worse from that point
on, as Vashti found herself haunted by the entire
concept of Phelan Keene's double-damned book.

She found herself hearing the interview over and
over in her mind, then wishing she'd had the facilities
to tape it, because she quickly became unsure of the
accuracy in her memory.

How old had the interview *really* been? Had he decided to write this book before her field audit on the
family business dealings? Or after? And was she to
be purely an accuracy consultant, or did he have far
more sinister plans for her involvement in the book?

The worries did nothing for Vashti's week and even
less for her weekend, especially when she found herself
face to face with Alana Keene in one of the city's
second-hand book shops just before Saturday noon.

'What have you been doing to my big brother?'
Alana asked, eyes wide with what Vashti thought
might be astonishment that anyone, female at least,

could be guilty of doing anything disagreeable to
Phelan Keene.

'I can't imagine,' she replied evasively, tucking a
copy of his very first book under her arm in the vain
hope that Alana might miss seeing it. 'Why? Is he
upset with me or something?'

'More *something*, I expect,' was the reply. 'He's
been going round for the past few days like somebody
kicked his dog. He's living alone out there in Dad's
old house, you know, and he really shouldn't be. I
think isolation is quite wrong for him, being a writer
and all. You've got to observe if you're going to write
about people, and out there the only thing to observe
is himself in the mirror. I finally had to leave in the
end, or else I'd have been saying something that would
have got *me* kicked.'

'Oh, surely not,' Vashti answered, not one bit sure
the remark was even half logical. Phelan Keene, she
suspected, might be capable of almost anything when
crossed.

'Figuratively speaking. He's a marshmallow, really,'
was the bright reply. And then, in a whisper that
carried like a cannon-shot through the shop, 'Surely
you're not going to *buy* that? I've got all his books
at home and I'd be more than happy to lend you one.

'Although,' she sniffed, 'that's the *last* of his books
you'd ever want to read. It's nothing but sex and violence and sex and violence and *more* sex and violence. His later stuff is much, much better.'

Vashti was caught floundering. Indeed this was the
'last' of his books she'd want to read; she'd already
read all the others, hoping against hope that he'd
already done the tax book he'd mentioned on the
radio. But she didn't dare tell Alana that!

'Well, if even his sister doesn't recommend it, perhaps I won't buy it after all,' she replied finally, only to contradict herself by then saying, 'Actually, I've got all his others, so yes, I will buy it.'

'Oh, not you too,' was the surprising reply, followed by a wide-eyed gasp. 'Open mouth; insert feet. I do a lot of that,' Alana said, shaking her head as if to deny any form of insult. 'I'm sorry, Vashti. It's just that every damned woman Phelan meets seems to fall for him like ... well ... you know! And he just laps it up like ... like it was his *due*.'

Alana stamped one small foot, her eyes bright with feeling. 'What my brother wants is a woman who'll give him a bash around the ear occasionally; he's had things all his own way for far too long.'

Vashti didn't know what to say, which was obvious to both girls. Alana suddenly grinned, saying, 'I do love him and he's really a wonderful person, deep down inside. But I'm afraid he's going to get spoiled even more rotten than he already is, if everybody in a skirt treats him like ... well, like that prize bitch Janice Gentry. Surely you saw that photo in the paper—she was all over him like a rash!'

Vashti had to laugh at the comparison between her own mental picture of leech-green and Alana's description. Then she had to explain her laughter—easy enough, because she truly did like Alana—then share it.

'He's leading a more dangerous life than I thought,' Alana said with a final giggle. 'Leeches and rashes and ... speak of the devil ...' She raised one eyebrow in a quick caution, but it was too late.

'Child sisters ought to have more respect,' said a familiar voice from behind Vashti.

She turned to look up into Phelan Keene's face, trying frantically to hide his book under her arm as she did so, but it was a futile gesture.

Long, tanned fingers reached out to pluck the book from her suddenly nerveless fingers.

'Shocking literary taste,' he growled, shaking his head in mock-dismay. 'And I suppose, having bought the thing second-hand—thus denying me my paltry royalties—you're going to expect me to autograph it.'

'I...was not.' Vashti managed to get out the denial, but she was wasting her breath. Phelan had already turned his attention to his sister.

'Give us a pen, little one,' he demanded, and was reaching out to accept the meekly provided object when Vashti managed to squeak,

'But I haven't even paid for it yet!'

'Oh! Well, you'd best do that first. Good thing you mentioned it, because of course an autographed copy would have cost you more,' he said sternly.

The book was thrust into her hands, then she was gripped by the shoulders, turned around, and quite forcibly shoved towards the cash register where a clerk—young, female and attractive—was staring wide-eyed at both the performance and at Phelan Keene.

Hardly surprising, Vashti thought as she hunched forward in an obvious attitude of self-consciousness. The man looked like an advertisement for a catalogue. His blue checked shirt was crisp and snug-fitting, as were the faded jeans he wore so well. His boots gleamed as brightly as the eyes that followed her. In the rather crowded confines of the small shop he loomed above the other browsers, fairly exuding a sort of roguish male vitality.

'Is that really...?' The sales clerk's whisper boomed through the quiet bookshop, her eyes never leaving the author as she took Vashti's money, rang up the sale, and counted the change.

Vashti didn't bother to answer. The photo on the dust-cover did that for her. All *she* wanted to do was somehow escape this ludicrous situation. But Phelan was watching too closely for that, unless she dared to just turn and flee, which would be adding insanity to ludicrousness, she thought.

To hell with it, she thought, and straightened her shoulders as she returned to where he and Alana stood waiting.

Suddenly aware of just how ratty she looked, in faded, paint-stained jeans and an over-sized sweatshirt, her hair gathered loosely at the back in a rubber band, Vashti went overboard in her reaction now to Phelan Keene's stirring.

'Please, sir,' she wheedled as she reached him, and slouched into a totally subservient posture. 'Please, sir, if I pay the royalty may I humbly beg that you autograph this book for me poor old granny? Please, sir! It'd mean so much to her, sir; she's one of your greatest fans.'

Fumbling into her handbag as Phelan took the book with a scowl, obviously taken aback by her performance, Vashti found a two cent copper, virtually obsolete because of the country's most recent currency changes, and had it ready when he returned the book to her after furiously scribbling inside it.

He handed her the book, accepted the coin without a glance, then *did* look at it, whereupon he fell into his own role with a vengeance, snarling, 'Foul little urchin . . . Get away with you. Your granny probably can't even read.'

Vashti took him at his word, and scuttled from the shop, only to find him right behind her, a hand outstretched to catch her by the shoulder before she could continue her escape. Alana, convulsed with laughter, was right behind him.

Phelan, however, wasn't laughing. He stood, hand still on Vashti's shoulder, his touch burning, she thought, right through the bulky fleece of the sweatshirt. His pale eyes, edged with the tiny wrinkles of a man much out of doors, gleamed with a message she couldn't read.

'You two should go on the stage; you make a great act,' bubbled Alana, apparently oblivious to the tension between them. Vashti, having to meet his eyes and squint because of the sun high in the sky behind him, was hardly conscious of his sister's presence.

'You look about twelve years old.' His voice rumbled down like distant thunder, barely audible and yet impossible not to hear. The message in his eyes was something far more complicated, too much so. Vashti couldn't think of an answer. She was caught by his gaze, held by it.

The sunlight in his dark, coarse, curly hair threw up rainbows, she thought, rainbows tinged with dark auburn. She found herself thinking that it was almost criminal for a man to have such long, thick eyelashes.

'If you two are going to stare into each others's eyes, how about doing it over coffee or something?' Alana's voice, liquid with suppressed laughter, flowed in to break the spell, if spell it had been. 'Or better yet, lunch! I vote we trot down to the botanical gardens; they do a scrumptious luncheon there.'

'Oh . . . no. I . . . well, look at me,' Vashti replied.

'You look fine. I'm only talking about lunch, not a reception at Government House.'

Vashti looked at the younger girl, casually dressed, to be sure, but neatly so, in jeans and riding boots and a plaid shirt beneath a jumper that matched her violet eyes.

'I look like a grot,' she replied. Firmly. Uselessly.

'Don't be silly. It's Saturday, after all. Not as if anybody's working or anything.'

'If I'm awake, I'm working!' Phelan joined the conversation for the first time.

'Oh, stop being so dogmatic, brother, dear,' Alana sniffed. 'You're doing no such thing, and anyway, it's Saturday.' She then ignored him, turning again to Vashti and casting an appraising eye.

'Well, I suppose I have to take your point, but it's no problem. We'll just whip you home for a quick change on the way.'

Vashti had no chance to reply.

'Not so fast, baby sister,' Phelan interrupted, reaching out to take Alana by the shoulder and turn her to face him. 'I have no objection to having Ms Sinclair join us for lunch; indeed I'd welcome it.' This was said with a wicked grin tossed in Vashti's direction. 'But not if you're going to start putting words in my mouth, or, even worse, ignoring what I say altogether. You do enough of that. So let me repeat— if I am awake, I am working! Doesn't matter if it's Saturday or Shrove Tuesday.'

'But why should it matter anyway? Honestly, Phelan, you do go on about the strangest things.'

'There's nothing strange about it,' he replied grimly. 'You forget, dear sister, that, while Ms Sinclair may be a darling girl, she is still *the enemy*.'

And he said it with such fierceness that both girls reared back in surprise.

'All the more reason to give it a miss,' Vashti snapped, the words pouring out in a torrent as she rushed to get her two bobs' worth in first.

'Oh, don't be silly,' Alana replied hotly, her words muddled with Phelan's, saying virtually the same thing.

'Maybe we can manage not to disagree so often if we have a neutral buffer, provided, of course, we can keep her quiet—which is seldom easy,' Phelan said then, taking each girl by the hand and turning to start off down the footpath. 'But we *are* going to eat, because arguing on an empty stomach is bad for the complexion. You lot mightn't have to worry, but I'm too old to take risks.'

He smiled at each girl in turn, then cast a sideways glance at Vashti, mischief lurking in his eyes. 'And I think we will stop and let you change, Ms Sinclair. I don't want you to feel at a disadvantage if the arguments get really interesting.'

Vashti allowed herself to be led along like, she thought, a lamb to the slaughter. And although she was on one side of the trio, she quickly felt as if she were square in the middle.

Phelan and his sister seemed to have agreed to disagree about anything and everything. Even as they walked to where Alana's car was parked—'No room for all three of us in that excut a paddock ute I'm reduced to driving,' Phelan said, adding, 'My temperament will improve out of sight when my own car arrives from the mainland next week'—the siblings argued and scrapped like a couple of ten-year-olds.

Vashti, an only child, found it a quite astonishing performance, not least so because, despite the fervent passions displayed, there was a clear thread of familial love and affection that never wavered.

She already knew that Alana shared a similar rapport with the elder brother, Bevan, but, he being a less volatile personality than Phelan, the relationship was less flamboyant.

How wonderful, though, she thought. Three children so vividly different in temperament and yet so united as a family despite their differences. Old Bede Keene must have been proud; each of his children in their own way had obviously lived up to his influence.

Memory of the old man sobered Vashti, and by the time they reached her flat she was half tempted to try once again to beg out of the luncheon.

But no chance.

'You've got five minutes to make yourself presentable,' Phelan remarked with a stern glance at his wristwatch. 'We won't come in; doesn't look like there'd be room for all three of us——' this with a grin that supposedly showed he was only joking '—but if you dilly-dally, I warn you, I'll come in and get you, ready or not!'

Vashti got out of the back seat and ran for the door of her flat. There was nothing else for it! Politeness should have required her to invite them in for a drink, or at least coffee, but Phelan hadn't been far off in saying there wasn't room. And she didn't have a drop of milk in the place, much less any sort of drink to offer.

She was back in seven minutes, the last two of which had been spent applying minimal make-up while keeping one eye on the door, as if Phelan Keene might be expected to kick it in like some marauding vandal.

Her grotty jeans were replaced by tidy trousers, the sweatshirt by a jersey blouse in shades of greys and pinks. Her hair, normally gathered in a tidy knot or braid for work, cried out for similar treatment today, but instead was quickly brushed and allowed to hang free.

There was hardly time to intellectualise the reasons; Vashti just knew she felt better and looked better with her hair free, though it was an extravagance she seldom allowed herself. It certainly wasn't, she determined, anything to do with Phelan Keene.

He was the most contrary individual, one day treating her as if she were, indeed, the *enemy*, only to switch attitudes without logic or warning and treat her as...well...*not* as the enemy, despite his remark. Not today—or at least not yet.

'Yet', she discovered upon her return to the car, was a relative term.

'If you were going to take *that* long, you could at least have worn legs,' Phelan muttered over his shoulder as she got into the rear of the car. He cast a disparaging look at her trousers, then glanced pointedly out of the front window as if to forestall any reply.

'You look lovely,' said his sister with a smile in the rear-view mirror. 'And you, brother, dear, should be grateful for such attractive company and keep your chauvinistic remarks to yourself.

'He doesn't mean them anyway,' she cried over her shoulder to Vashti. 'It's just part of his ''Aren't I wonderful?—I'm a famous writer" role. He doesn't think it's proper to be a real, human man and write all that sex-and-chauvinism macho rubbish at the same time.'

'Girls with good legs shouldn't be allowed to wear trousers,' Phelan retorted firmly. 'It's all right for you; you've got fat ankles, and you're my sister anyway. I have to put up with you.'

'You have to put up with both of us,' Alana replied without taking her eyes off the road as she squealed into a minuscule hole in the traffic. 'So put a lid on it, or I'll throw my ladylike manners to the wind and we'll treat Vashti to a real Keene domestic over lunch.'

Phelan shrugged, obviously bored, and having made his point anyway. 'Just don't throw away your rudimentary driving skills,' he muttered. 'I'd like to get there in one piece, if it's all the same to you.'

'*He* taught me to drive,' Alana replied, turning to grin over the seat-back at Vashti.

'Only enough for you to sneak a pass out of an examiner who was blind-drunk at the time,' Phelan said, bracing himself as she flew into the railway roundabout like a rally driver.

'The examiner,' Alana confided over her shoulder with seemingly total inattention to the road ahead, 'quite liked my ankles.'

They swept round the back of the Domain and into the botanical gardens car park, where Phelan emerged from the vehicle, giving thanks to St Christopher, and only—or so it seemed—helping Vashti out of the car as a sort of second thought.

But there was nothing secondary about the way he swept his gaze over her figure as she emerged, nor about the look in his eye as he held her fingers in a firm, over-long grasp.

And when he gallantly took a girl on each arm and declared, 'I'll be the envy of every bloke in the place,' as he marched them towards the restaurant, Vashti didn't know what to make of him. Especially as she thought she heard a muttered 'Even in trousers' under his breath.

She was treated to what, for her, was a rare example of sibling bantering, throughout a splendid lunch, and Vashti kept finding herself thinking how lucky both Phelan and Alana were.

An only child herself, she found their constant point-scoring confusing at first, then realised it was simply their way of expressing very deep emotions while sharpening their wits at the same time.

She'd have been content just to sit back and enjoy the performance, except that both kept trying to draw her into their games, which would have been fine if she'd known how, known the rules. But the whole thing was quite beyond her experience, and Vashti finally had to say so.

'An only child? Your poor thing,' was Alana's immediate response. 'Not that there haven't been moments in my young life when I'd have envied you.' Then, with sudden seriousness, 'But not very many.'

'You're talking rubbish,' Phelan declared, throwing a very strange look across the table at Vashti. 'At least she'll be able to grow up and marry without making some poor fool's life a living hell.'

'You're a fine one to talk,' retorted his sister. 'You're *never* going to grow up, and any woman who'd have you wants her head read! Thirty-six years old and he still spends half his life in fantasy-land,' she continued with a quirky grin to Vashti. 'He writes about all these macho heroes and busty, steamy heroines and then gets round with a...an accountant!'

'Now hang about!' Phelan snapped. 'There's no call to get personal.' Then his scowl vanished, replaced by a broad knowing grin. 'And don't forget that our Ms Sinclair is an accountant, so watch your mouth, little sister.'

'Vashti is a person, not a walking calculator,' Alana replied, totally undismayed by her *faux pas*.

Vashti squirmed in her chair, wishing frantically for the waitress to return on any excuse, just to stop this line of discussion before it went any further.

Phelan, on the other hand, was clearly enjoying seeing her squirm.

'*All* women have calculating minds, so you'll have to be more specific than that. What have you got against accountants, anyway?' he demanded of his sister.

'You're a filthy chauvinist pig,' was the fiery response, drawing only a laugh, which even Vashti had to share.

'That round clearly goes to...Mr Keene,' she said haltingly, flustered at having nearly used his first name while so aware that he was insisting on not using hers.

'See what I mean?' he immediately asked, adding to her confusion. And his eyes twinkled with satisfaction as he declared, 'Vashti—obviously a woman of splendid breeding and exemplary manners— couldn't bring herself to call me Phelan on such short acquaintance, and is far too refined to call me a chauvinist pig, so her calculating mind took over and came up with a proper compromise.'

'She was just being polite.'

'Was she?'

'No!' declared Vashti, suddenly embarrassed and just a bit exasperated by being talked about as if she weren't even there. '*She* is going to the loo. And when *she* gets back, *she* will expect to have coffee and a change of subject, or *she* is going home.'

Whereupon *she* left the table and practically ran from the room, not sure whether to be truly hurt or insulted by it all, but dead sure she needed a break from Phelan Keene's persistent scrutiny.

Even when he'd been in full-bore verbal war with his sister, the man had used his eyes more as weapons against Vashti.

Without lifting a finger, he'd stroked her hair, caressed the long line of her throat, undone each and every button on her blouse and skilfully touched her nipples to an exquisite tenderness.

And by lifting only one finger, he'd quietly hitched up her glasses to ensure that she was unable to miss seeing exactly what he was up to.

Removing the hateful glasses, she splashed cold water into her eyes and stared at her reflection in the mirror. Her nipples still tingled from Phelan's gaze, and despite the excellent meal she felt empty, hollow, hungry. Stupid, she thought. Stupid to feel this way; stupid to be here in the first place.

'And stupid to let him *get* to you like that!' she snarled with a scowl at the myopic image before her.

She returned to the table determined to drink her coffee, pay her share of the bill, and then leave. It wasn't a long walk home across the Domain, and walking would do her good.

But when Phelan stood up at her approach and walked round to hold her chair for her, she found herself too readily noticing the easy, cat-like grace of the man, and when he smiled and said quietly after returning to sit down, 'My sister apologises,'—making not the slightest gesture of apology himself—she didn't know whether to laugh or cry.

Alana ignored him. 'I have to behave,' she said with a ten-year-old's scowl. 'Or he says he'll put me in a book. That's his *direst* threat, you know? And what's worse—he means it. You'll see, when you get round to reading that heap of sadistic garbage you bought this morning.'

She leaned across the table, ignoring Phelan as if he didn't exist, weren't there, weren't listening. 'I'm in *all* his books, but I never get anything exciting to do, never get any of the really dishy men, or the hot-shot lovers. I *did* get killed once, but that's about it. Such a boring existence.'

Vashti couldn't help it. She erupted with laughter so intense that it brought tears to her eyes and an ache to her over-stuffed empty-feeling stomach.

Because of course it was true! She hadn't picked it up, but probably would have; there had been something vaguely familiar about Alana ever since Vashti had read the first of Phelan's epics. Now she realised what it was.

She laughed, then laughed some more, deliberately not looking at Phelan, not daring to include him in what had suddenly become a girls-only joke.

'But surely you *enjoy* it?' she asked in a serious deadpan, leaning across to meet Alana's secretive gaze. 'I realise being killed isn't much fun, but surely the fame, the recognition . . .'

'It's all right, I suppose. But you know what really gets on my wick?' Alana hissed in a conspiratorial whisper. Vashti, wide-eyed now and quite revelling in her part, sat with lips parted in anticipation.

Alana's voice dropped even further. 'The man's colour-blind! Or else he's just got no taste; I'm not sure which. So I ended up being dead in clothes you wouldn't be caught dead in!'

'Next time, you'll go in fat ankles and all; I've spared you that so far at least,' Phelan threatened now, too obviously trying to control his own chuckles.

His sister was totally nonplussed. Vashti could only sit with bated breath for the explosion she thought *must* come if this continued much further.

'Well, what about Vashti, then?' Alana demanded. 'You can't give *her* fat ankles; she'd have you jailed for tax evasion.'

Vashti felt her heart leap, her every cautionary instinct alert, poising her to flee, given half a chance.

But she couldn't, could only sit like a mesmerised prey animal, awaiting her fate. Every fear, every trepidation about Phelan's plans for the book with her involvement soared into flight inside her skull, making a roaring sound so loud that she could barely hear him reply.

'She might anyway,' Phelan mused, now turning his gaze once again to caress Vashti's throat. 'No, for Vashti I'd have to leave everything just exactly as it is. Even——' with one finger at the bridge of his nose '—the glasses.'

His eyes, oblivious to his sister's interest, moved lower, caressing Vashti's breasts with obvious pleasure. 'Except I don't think I could kill her off as easily as I did you. It would have to be *seduction*, with perhaps a touch of revenge involved, I think. Heavy on the seduction.'

'Thank goodness for that,' Vashti heard herself saying, wondering that she could speak at all for the turmoil inside her. And, astonished, continued. 'I mean, with the price of nail polish today, torture would be just *so* expensive.'

No mention of the torture already endured, the promise she read in his eyes of more—*far* more—to come. There was no longer any question in her mind; Phelan's alleged book was no more than an excuse. He was out to get her, and didn't mind what methods he used in the process.

'I'll remember that,' Phelan said, signalling for the account. And his eyes told her he definitely would.

So she was instantly on guard when they got outside and Phelan suggested Alana leave he and Vashti to walk off their lunch.

'We can have a good look at the gardens and then it's not that far through the Domain to where the ute's parked,' he suggested. 'Or I might even *walk* you home, if you're game.'

The offer was too sudden, too unexpected. Her instincts told her to refuse, but weren't quick enough to stop her tongue.

'I think that might be very nice,' Vashti found herself saying, feeling yet again that impossible feeling of emptiness in her tummy.

'You watch him,' was Alana's parting remark, made without, Vashti couldn't help noticing, the slightest hint of any argument. 'He'll be all shirty because we ganged up on him, and he's likely as not to get frisky on a full stomach. Just remember you won't be able to run very fast with tidy little ankles like that.'

'Racehorses do,' Vashti replied with a grin, and added, with a bravery she certainly didn't feel, 'Besides, could it possibly be *worse* than being put in a *book*?'

Which got her a speculative glance from Alana and a waved farewell; she didn't dare look to see Phelan's reaction.

Her own reactions concerned Vashti quite enough by themselves, starting the instant he took her hand in his and said, one eyebrow cocked in sardonic amusement, 'I've always wanted to be a jockey.'

CHAPTER FOUR

PHELAN continued to hold her hand, rather to Vashti's surprise, as he led her off into the Royal Botanical Gardens.

And he kept holding her hand—not that she was terribly disposed to have it back—as they wandered amid the vast array of trees and shrubs.

'I haven't seen these new Japanese gardens,' he said, thus breaking a rather long silence as they walked. Vashti hadn't either, but didn't say so. For some reason, the need to talk had been lessened with Alana's departure; she was content just to stroll and enjoy the experience in silence.

It wasn't until they paused on the bright scarlet bridge in the Japanese gardens, both of them staring down into the tranquil runs of water between the rock waterfalls, that words seemed necessary.

'I really envy you your family,' Vashti said without looking up at Phelan. 'It comes of my being an only child, I suppose, but you're all so... so vibrant, and so strongly supportive, even if you do pretend to bicker all the time.'

'What do you mean—"pretend"?' he scoffed. 'We do bicker all the time. Or at least Alana and I do. And she's even worse with Bevan, because he's more the strong, silent type, and my dear child sister simply can't *abide* silence, I sometimes think.'

'I quite like her,' Vashti replied.

63

'Which means what? That you don't like me? Or that you're not saying?'

She looked up to see one dark eyebrow cocked in amusement, and was suddenly only too aware of the hand that was captive in his lean, strong fingers.

'You really like a good stir,' she replied evasively, making the reply more question than comment.

'Of course.'

'It's not something I'm very good at.'

'Except over the phone, I've noticed.' And once again that eyebrow went up.

'It must help to have a good memory,' she quickly blurted.

'And you don't?'

'Only for figures,' Vashti replied, and then flinched at the innuendo as Phelan ensured she couldn't free her hand.

'Now you're even stealing my lines,' he chuckled. 'You don't need a great memory if you can read minds. And you don't have to be embarrassed about it, either.'

'I'm not,' she lied, then found herself stuck for words as she contemplated what he'd really said. It was too easy to remember when she'd thought he was the one able to read minds—or her own, at least, which was the problem.

But now she was faced with a quite different problem as Phelan turned to stand close to her, taking full advantage of the bridge rail at her back.

'You reckon you can read my mind now?' he asked, and his voice, though soft, echoed like surf in her head. His pale eyes seemed to expand until they were all she could see, as he lowered his mouth to capture her lips.

Vashti's first reaction had been to twist away, to somehow escape this intimacy she both wanted and feared. But his hands were on the rail, holding her body immobile without ever quite touching her. Only their lips touched, and his kiss was gentle, undemanding.

Vashti's lips parted, accepting his kiss without really replying to it. Her instinctive need to lift her arms, to touch him, was forestalled by an equally instinctive caution that thrust through her mind with his own words tumbling over and over and over. 'The enemy... enemy... enemy...'

But in her mouth was the taste of him, sharp and clean, in her nostrils the faint scent of his aftershave. No enemy taste, no enemy scent.

And then his hands were on her waist, pulling her closer to him, and her own hands were lifted, pressed between them in a barrier that did nothing against the warmth and firmness of his body.

She could feel his arousal as his hand slid down to hold her hips tight against him, and now his kiss was firmer, demanding a response she couldn't hide or deny.

'Vashti...' His voice was soft, a whisper lifting from his tongue as her mouth parted to accept his deeper kiss. Under her fingers she could feel the muscles flex as he breathed, could feel his nipples firm to her involuntary exploration.

Madness, this! As his lips left her mouth to trace a path of shuddering torment along her cheek, then down along the arched hollow of her throat, she couldn't stop herself twisting to ease his way. Her hands, thrusting against the muscles of his chest, were no barrier to the lips that wandered unerringly down the front of her blouse, much less to the fingers that now had slid beneath it and were lightly rippling upwards along the nubbles of her spine.

The gasping of her own breath thundered inside her head, the sound mingling with the warmth of his breath as it sighed and sang beside her ear. And with all, another sound—that of children's voices raised in play.

Vashti was struggling to free herself even as that noise became evident, struggling so fiercely that she almost tipped over the bridge railing as Phelan also heard, and stopped his plunder of her senses.

Her eyes blazing with embarrassment and anger, she had her blouse tucked in again and was running desperate fingers through her hair, not daring to look at Phelan, hardly daring to open her eyes, when the children gambolled into view from behind the French Memorial Fountain.

And when she did look up, it was to meet laughing, ice-green eyes that danced with what she could only construe as satisfaction.

It took her several deep breaths to recover any semblance of composure, to calm the waves of sensuous passion and fiery rage that surged side by side through her body. Her legs felt like limp ropes; without the railing to hang on to, she would surely have collapsed at the feet of this horrid, laughing man.

'I'm sure you think it's hilarious,' she finally managed to snarl. 'Saved by the laughter of the little children? How frightfully convenient! What chapter is that supposed to be, I wonder?'

Phelan met her glare squarely, his eyes darker now, somehow, totally unreadable except for the vestiges of passion that flared like sunspots against his irises.

'What are——?' He got no further before Vashti flung herself past his relaxed arm and stalked away, unwilling to hear his answer, wanting only to get away from the turbulence of his presence.

Her heels clattered on the bridge deck, then thudded along the pathway as she surged forward, head down, intent only on escape. But he was beside her in mere strides, and there he stayed as she plunged along the track, oblivious to her direction.

And he stayed beside her, not touching her, not speaking, but moving with cat-like grace, easily keeping up, and hovering like an extra shadow. Vashti tried to ignore his presence, couldn't, tried to freeze him by sheer force of will, failed.

And in the end she halted, breathing as quickly and frantically as she had in his arms. But not now with the unchecked warmth of his body against her; now she was icy-cold and shivering, despite the relative warmth of the day.

'You . . . you . . .' She couldn't even find the words, though they scurried inside her head like so many bumper-cars, bouncing off each other without pattern.

'I'm a rotter, I know,' he said with a half-grin. 'Or should we try something really literary, like "depraved lecher" or "scoundrel"? I've always quite liked "scoundrel", although I can't remember ever using it. Good lord, woman, what's so horribly awful about a stolen kiss in a park?'

The question stunned her into silence, thwarting the savage reply that had been forming on her lips.

Stolen kiss? Compared to her own feelings of having been literally *controlled*, it sounded so...so little. But in reality, she thought, what else had it been? She had indeed been kissed, but he hadn't actually touched her in any way that could be described as intimate. Except that he *had*! He'd touched her with great intimacy, but the touch had been in her mind, in her very being.

And she couldn't possibly describe, or indeed *admit*, just how intimate that touch had been, couldn't let him realise how easily he'd breached her defences, how he'd stirred feelings she hadn't *wanted* stirred.

'Stolen kiss? Is that what it was?' she demanded scathingly. 'That's a pretty simple description for some quite juvenile groping, I'd have thought. And I am not particularly impressed by such antics, *Mr* Keene, unlike your fictional heroines.'

'Ah.' He breathed the word softly, almost thoughtfully, as he stood at a respectful distance, meeting her fiery gaze with eyes as calm and still as glacial tarns.

His stare seemed to go on forever, as if he felt the calmness in his own eyes could somehow bridge the almost tangible link with her own.

'Especially,' he said then, still speaking so softly that she could barely hear, 'in public.'

'At all!' Vashti replied, trying to force into her voice a firmness she didn't quite feel. Damn the man anyway! All he had to do was look at her, and she could feel her resolve weakening.

'OK.' The reply was too quick, too simple. 'No more juvenile groping. And I apologise; I should have known better.'

The admission and the totally unexpected apology left her weaponless, not to mention speechless. She could only stand there and force herself to meet his eyes—eyes that now glimmered with hidden laughter, eyes that denied both admission and apology while forcing her to accept both.

'Let's continue on our way, then, shall we?' he finally said, and turned along the path towards the tropical glasshouse and the cactus house. Vashti, her anger with Phelan defused and her anger with herself boiling furiously but undisclosable, paused only a moment before joining his casual stroll.

They walked for half an hour in a sort of rigid silence, a situation that grew increasingly uncomfortable for Vashti. She kept seeing things she wanted to share, but stubbornly held to the seemingly agreed silence. Her anger had faded against the spectacular beauty in the tropical displays and the manifold shapes and colours of the cacti.

Only when Phelan paused on the bridge at the tranquil lily pond did a flicker of her former anger emerge, but it couldn't be sustained, not even when she stumbled in the cool depths of the fern house and his fingers leapt to steady her, only to release her with an unexpected suddenness before she could even think to object.

And even as she murmured her thanks, it was to his moving flank, drawing only a sort of grunted acceptance.

'This is stupid.' Vashti stepped up her pace, thrusting herself around to halt him, making him face her.

'What is?' The question belied the glimmer of amusement in pale eyes, an amusement made all the more obvious by one dark eyebrow cocked to reveal it.

'This . . . this attitude! That's what.'

'Attitude? My attitude—or yours?' Now his eyes actually laughed; even his voice chuckled behind a wry half-grin.

'Ours, if that makes it any easier,' Vashti replied sternly. She was giving in, and knew it, but the alternative was a day totally ruined, and she didn't fancy that.

'If we keep going on like this it's going to ruin the whole day for both of us,' she insisted. 'And I . . . I don't want that. I really enjoyed lunch and, well, I don't want the day to end on a sour note, that's all.'

'Ah,' Phelan said, again drawing out the sound as he held her eyes with his own. 'But the day isn't over yet, is it? Who knows what's yet to come?'

'Well, I just wanted to say that I'm sorry I overreacted back there; that's all.' Vashti had to drop her eyes to make the admission, but make it she must. She was not and never had been a vengeful person, and found it impossible to remain angry for any length of time.

'OK. And I'm sorry I gave you cause,' he replied soberly. 'Although I'm not one damned bit sorry I kissed you, even if I did apologise. You're far too pretty not to be kissed. I may even——' with a roguish grin '—do it again some time, and you can decide for yourself whether that's a threat or a promise.'

'Definitely a threat,' Vashti replied lightly, trying to maintain the conversation in a light-hearted vein.

And she felt a curious little lurch in her tummy when he grinned and replied, 'Only in public. And if we walk much further without a break, even that threat would be hollow, because I'd be too tired to be threatening. Come sit down in this wondrously named Wombat One picnic shelter and tell me the story of your life.'

'I'd much rather listen to the story of yours,' Vashti replied, thankfully moving into the shade. 'My life story's far too boring to bother with.'

Which, in her own mind, it was. Only somehow it didn't seem so under Phelan Keene's gentle but skilled probing. She found herself revealing more than she realised, especially when he adroitly turned the subject to her work.

They had left the botanical gardens and climbed up the steep slope to the children's playground and then downslope again towards Cleary's Gates before Vashti realised just how *much* Phelan had been pumping her about her job and the way things really worked in the taxation office, and the realisation made her stop dead in her tracks.

'I suppose you've been told before that you're cunning and devious and very, very clever at questioning people,' she charged. 'But I can tell you now that there's nothing to be gained by it.'

Which was as far as she dared go without coming out with a direct accusation that he was quizzing her merely to gather material for the book, that he really didn't care that much about Vashti herself, about how she felt, about how she feared his interest, feared for her privacy.

'That's what you think,' replied Phelan as they reached the edge of the busy Brooker Highway. Then he reached out to take her hand as he briskly gauged the traffic in both directions. 'But now isn't the time to yammer on about it; come on, before one of us gets run over.'

They dashed to the centre barricade, then on to the top of Stoke Street. By the time they'd wended their way through north Hobart to where Phelan had parked his utility, Vashti had mostly forgotten her concerns, deciding she'd told him nothing compromising anyway.

But a different caution took hold with his offer then to drive her home. If he did that, she'd have to invite him in for coffee—but she had no milk in the flat—or a drink—she didn't have a drop except for some aged cooking sherry—or...

'I'll only have time to just drop you off and maybe share a very quick coffee if you'd be so kind. I've got somewhere I have to stop before I head back to the farm,' he said, as if reading her mind. And if so, could he read the turmoil there? The incident in the park notwithstanding, she felt at least reasonably comfortable with Phelan here on the street.

But to be quite honest with herself, the thought of having him in her tiny flat, where his dominant personality would be overwhelming...

'All right, then, but I'll have to impose on you to stop so I can get some milk,' she replied, safe now in the implications of his remark.

She was leaving the milk bar, having decided on the spur of the moment to pig out on some rich chocolate biscuits as well, and was crossing the street to where Phelan was parked when the blast of sports-car exhaust warned her to leap back on the footpath.

'Fool!' she muttered, only half conscious that the passenger in the low-slung machine appeared strikingly familiar.

Phelan, having noticed the incident, was scowling into his rear-view mirror when Vashti slid into the passenger seat, but if he too had recognised Janice Gentry it went unmentioned.

It wasn't until they'd arrived in front of Vashti's flat that his scowl totally disappeared, but he was positively beaming when he walked round to open the utility's door for her.

'Now that you've got milk and bikkies, I reckon that cup of coffee would go down extremely well,' he said, his pale eyes a vision of innocence, backed up by the broad grin.

'I thought you had somewhere you had to be?' she replied hastily, forcing a smile of her own to cover the sinking feeling in the pit of her stomach. Of course he'd had somewhere else to go—until he'd seen that Janice Gentry wasn't about to be there!

'I did, but I've decided it wasn't that important after all,' he replied. And his bland expression covered what she assumed must be bitter disappointment.

She tried not to show her own disappointment as she met his smile and said brightly, 'All right, then, but you'll have to promise to behave.'

And could have kicked herself! What stupidity, to be instigating word games with this man after the day's earlier incident. But Phelan, as if perceiving her uncertainty, only nodded. Then he held up one hand, fingers crossed, and shot her one of those devastating little-boy grins.

It wasn't until they were inside the flat that he reached out, impishly, to push her glasses up into place, saying, 'You worry far too much, Vashti,' then turned away before she could reply and began to prowl the small lounge room while Vashti put the kettle on and began to spoon out the instant coffee.

She watched silently as he moved blatantly through the room, peering at her small collection of paintings, her records, and her eclectic range of books. These filled almost every available space in the small flat, and Phelan was still inspecting them when the water had boiled.

He glanced up to meet her enquiring eyes, then grinned hugely and remarked, 'I suppose it's rude of me, but nosing through other people's bookshelves is one habit I've never been able to break.'

'I don't mind,' she replied. 'It would hardly be fair, considering that's one bad habit we share.'

'Aha! Something in common. Now, at least, we've got a place to start.'

'What *are* you talking about?' She set the tray down on the coffee-table, then moved to sit in a single chair, leaving the couch to Phelan.

'Our relationship, of course. Or didn't you think we were going to have one?' There was mischief in his pale eyes now, and the start of a grin, as he sprawled on to the couch and reached for his coffee, waving a rejection of the milk and sugar.

'I'll have a bikkie, though. If you have to get through them all by yourself you're liable to get fat, and we wouldn't want that. Would we?'

'What relationship?' Vashti ladled more sugar than usual into her own coffee, suspiciously holding Phelan's mocking gaze as she did so.

'Ah,' he replied. 'Well, now, we'll just have to wait and see about that, I reckon.' But the look in his eyes said something quite different. There was again that slightly predatory gleam as his eyes moved to touch her lips, to prowl the long expanse of her throat.

'I do wish you'd stop that,' she protested, hoping the protest would distract him from noticing the effect he was having on her. Even before his eyes had reached her breasts, Vashti was aware of how her nipples were firming, were tingling, almost as if he were touching them with his lips, his fingers.

'Stop looking at you? Whatever for?' And his grin was almost smug now. 'I enjoy looking at you, dear Vashti, and I intend to do it every chance I get.'

Then the smugness was replaced by an obviously overdone expression of pensiveness as he complained, 'Although I would prefer it if you'd give up wearing trousers; that's almost a crime with legs like yours.'

'You are incorrigible,' Vashti retorted, unable to repress a chuckle at his deliberate put-on. 'How would you feel if I started laying down the law to you about what you wear?'

'Is that in the nature of a complaint?' And his grin became decidedly devilish as she shook her head without thinking. She had never seen him, either casually, as now, or when dressed up, as he'd been for the funeral and for business meetings, when his clothes hadn't fitted to perfection and suited him equally well. And he knew it, the rotter!

'And you've never even seen *my* legs,' he chuckled. 'Yet.' Those self-same legs, snugly encased in his trousers, seemed to stretch halfway across her lounge, and Vashti didn't need to see them to know their strength, to recall the feel of them against her as he'd held her close to him.

'I do wish you'd stop trying to work up these fictional scenarios,' she said, the crossness in her voice more put on than real. 'You insist on mistaking facts for fiction, which is a truly ridiculous way to go about things.'

'Oh, I know the difference. Don't let my baby sister steer you wrong on that score,' he replied. Then, before Vashti could think to reply, 'And we're *not* going to talk business now and ruin a perfectly enjoyable afternoon, not when we're already scheduled to meet on Monday and finish off this damned family tax audit thing. For now, there are far more pleasant subjects, had we only the time to explore them.'

Draining his coffee, he was on his feet in a single, lithe movement. 'Thank you for that. Now I'd best go or you'll be having me for dinner as well as lunch, which might be altogether too much of a good thing.'

He turned in the doorway and reached out with a long forefinger to push Vashti's glasses back into place, grinning as she frowned at him for doing so. Then his finger traced a slow path down along her cheek and the side of her mouth before lifting her chin just enough so that he could bend down and kiss her. It was a brief kiss, light and gentle, as one might give a child, yet it somehow held a promise untold, a promise added to by his quirky grin.

'Been a lovely day,' he said quietly. 'But on Monday, wear legs; on Monday it's back to battle stations.'

Vashti had no chance to reply, could only watch as he moved down the footpath in his long, countryman's strides to get into his utility and drive off without so much as a wave.

She spent that evening quietly, reading his first novel and realising why Alana had advised her against buying it. By comparison with his later work it was rough indeed, yet already showing the complicated, tortuous mind of the author.

Throughout Sunday, that contrariness of Phelan Keene's haunted Vashti's own mind. One minute so friendly, the next too friendly by half, and yet just as quick to turn angry and savage, to withdraw into himself at some real or fancied slight she couldn't understand at all.

None of which, she thought, should be bothering her at all. She was, after all, in a relative position of power; whatever devious approach Phelan Keene or, more likely, Janice Gentry might dream up, it was *she* who had the vast powers of the taxation act to back her up.

But she slept poorly on Sunday night, her restlessness only added to by flickering nightmares that melted to nothing each time they woke her, leaving no memory of their content. When the alarm finally forced her awake, she felt haggard and looked worse.

'Power dressing; that's what's called for here,' she told the hollow-eyed image in her mirror, judiciously applying more make-up than usual to make that image appear bright-eyed and alert. Her hair went into its usual neat French roll.

'Power dressing ... and legs!' She muttered the words like some sort of incantation as she sorted through her meagre wardrobe. It didn't take long; her best black shoes were in being mended, which left only the best grey ones. Her 'best' black suit was at the cleaner's anyway, and for the image she wanted today the soft dove-grey with the flaring lapels was probably better anyway, especially over the high-necked white silk blouse she had bought specifically to go with it. The skirt was perhaps a bit short, but all the experts had been predicting a return for the mini, she thought with a wan smile. And as for legs, she had one pair of tights that were perfect, with an almost invisible pattern that only enhanced their sheen.

She ignored breakfast—except for her mandatory three cups of coffee—and was ready early enough for a leisurely walk to work, carrying both raincoat and new umbrella just in case.

En route, she collected her morning papers and an egg and bacon roll, which she consumed carefully at her desk, ever aware of how the soft grey suit would stain. The papers told her nothing the radio at home had not; the egg and bacon roll sat like lead in her stomach.

And there just wasn't any reason for it! The work had been done; there wasn't a case to be answered, only a few final details to be tidied up and approved. But Vashti was tense, leery of what was to come. Janice Gentry—and if anyone was to blame for the confusion in the Keene family tax matters it was that woman—would be unable to put the matter to rest without some final blow, Vashti thought.

She was certain of it by the appointed deadline, but rather less sure why Phelan Keene and his accountant were late. And when they did arrive, complete with apology, she found herself wishing they'd been later still—like at least a full day later!

Janice Gentry's version of power dressing was almost identical to Vashti's own, but there was no compliment in that—not when it was so obvious to any feminine eye that the tall brunette was the one wearing the designer 'original', both in the soft grey suit and high-necked silk blouse and even the general style of the matching shoes. Just one of the shoes would have paid for Vashti's outfit, costly as it had been on a working girl's budget.

Vashti's heart sank to join the leaden egg and bacon roll, helped on its way by the smug raising of one elegant dark eyebrow as Ms Gentry swept into the office murmuring a self-satisfied greeting.

If Phelan Keene, himself elegantly turned out in a perfectly tailored suit and a crisp white shirt that glistened against his tan, even noticed the similarity in the women's outfits, he gave no indication of it.

He greeted Vashti with a smile that was no more than polite, took the seat offered him, and leaned back in it as if to distance himself from the ensuing fireworks.

For her part, Vashti found herself merely taking a deep breath and plunging into discussion of the issues; delaying would accomplish nothing, she thought, so why not get it over with as soon as possible?

Janice Gentry countered almost immediately with a list of complaints—not one of them relevant—about the entire affair. With Phelan there, she was clearly playing to a captive audience, and her litany sounded—must have sounded, Vashti thought—quite valid and even logical. But there was no logic in it, and both girls knew it all too well.

Phelan Keene sat in silence, offering no explanations and being asked for none. He was doing, Vashti admitted beneath her growing frustration, exactly what she'd advised him to do—letting his adviser do what she was paid to do.

And throughout the performance—Vashti was certain it was no more than that, on Janice Gentry's part—lay a growing thread of accusation aimed not at the taxation office, but at herself.

She had missed it, at first, her attention admittedly divided by wondering just what part Phelan himself planned to take in all this. But as his silence continued, she found herself more and more aware that the elegant accountant was leading the discussion deliberately into the highly subjective field of simple harassment.

And Phelan was helping her, if only through his silence. He still took no active part in the verbal exchange, but where his eyes had held that element of distance, even of amusement, now they were icy and cold.

Vashti floundered, unsure of her ground now and not willing to let the arguments degenerate into something totally counter-productive. 'I think we're getting well off the subject here,' she finally said, starting to rise to her feet in a bid to end the interview somehow, anyhow.

She had to! With her attention divided between the Gentry woman's insidious, deliberate sniping and Phelan Keene's now almost threatening silence, she was in real danger of making what could be a serious professional mistake.

Help did come, however, if from the most surprising quarter.

'I think it's time we gave this a rest,' Phelan suddenly interjected, speaking virtually for the first time since he'd entered the room. 'We're starting to go round in circles now, and it's accomplishing damn-all.'

'But Phelan, *darling*.' Janice Gentry's voice was suddenly dove-soft, her mouth almost pouting as she turned her attention from Vashti to focus it upon Phelan.

But it was her words, not the change of attention, that captured Vashti, pinning her in her chair and stunning her to a silence that illogically roared in her ears.

'We are not just going in circles. It's just this kind of frivolous harassment, you know, that sent your father to his grave.'

The words seemed to zoom around the office, taking on a life of their own and increasing in volume. It was like a nightmare, a vortex of sound, a cyclone of accusation.

Vashti's breath seemed caught inside her chest; she felt as if she were gasping, drowning. Her own feelings of anger, surprise—indeed, astonishment—combined to keep her mute, to make it impossible to do anything except stare from Phelan Keene to his companion, hearing the accusation over and over again, but unable to really comprehend.

How could this woman *say* such a thing? Even *think* it? And how could Phelan Keene, the man who only yesterday, it seemed, had shared a meal with her, laughed with her, *kissed* her—how could he...?

'That's as it may be, but this isn't the time to get into it.' His voice echoed in Vashti's ears as if coming from some great distance. She forced herself to look at him, to meet those predatory eyes. He *couldn't* believe this...not possibly...

But he did! The belief fairly radiated in the chill look that met her pleading eyes. And suddenly she knew the reason behind his antagonism at their very first meeting, when he'd plundered her with his devilish wolf eyes in the bleak little churchyard on that lonely ridge.

This man truly *believed* she had harassed his father into the grave! Vashti's stomach churned just at the thought, and even as she tried to rise from her chair, tried to summon up the words of denial, she felt a curious light-headedness, knew she couldn't stand, much less speak. Her bottom seemed glued to the seat; her lips seemed glued to each other, despite being parted in what seemed a continual gasping for breath.

Phelan Keene was on his feet now, looking at her curiously while gesturing to Janice Gentry. He might even have been speaking, but Vashti couldn't hear the words through the roaring in her head, couldn't seem to see the expression in his eyes, because her own vision was swimming, blurred.

She could only sense the movement as her rival gathered up papers and moved in a blur of grey towards the office door. There was a change of light as the door opened and shut, closing off the sound of the accusation but not the horrible, gut-wrenching shock of it.

Vashti let her head sink into her hands, and allowed the new silence to wash over her as she gasped and gulped for air, in one second afraid she'd be ill, the next certain of it.

It all just seemed so impossible! She hadn't harassed Phelan's father; she had liked, perhaps even *loved* the old man, had certainly known and respected him as a person of great integrity. How anyone could even *think* otherwise—how *Phelan* could possibly think otherwise, close as he was to his brother and sister...

She didn't hear the door to her office open again, only sensed she was no longer alone when his voice, feather-soft, penetrated her shell of agony.

'I just wanted you to know that... that wasn't my idea,' he said. 'It was... nasty and uncalled-for.'

'Get out!'

Her own voice was as soft as his, almost a whisper in the quiet of the office. But it was tinged with steel, forged in the fires of her agony, her disgust. Phelan started to speak, indeed stepped further towards her as he did so.

'I said get out. Now!'

Vashti couldn't bear it. His very presence, despite his assurances, only served to add weight to the accusations, to the soul-destroying *evil* of the accusations. She hated it, hated it all—hated Janice Gentry, hated Phelan Keene, hated his words, his very existence.

'Out!'

Her voice was louder now, demanding, insisting. She half rose from her chair, fingers clenched around the bulk of her penholder, a solid obelisk of marble. The violence of her feelings had her shaking; she drew back her hand without any certainty of whether she might throw the penholder at him or simply bash him with it, but she would do something . . . something violent!

'We have to talk about——'

'I said *get out*.' Now her voice was ice itself, frozen as her feelings, brittle as her sudden feelings of loathing. Phelan met her eyes, ignoring the impromptu weapon in her hand. His own eyes were bleak, but it was a different bleakness from that of their first encounter, though Vashti couldn't have explained the difference, only knew it was so.

'Of course.' His words were almost self-defeating, caught by the barrier between them and hurled to nothingness. But he seemed not to notice as he turned and walked away, pausing in the doorway only to look back at Vashti, shaking his head in a tiny, silent gesture before he closed the door behind him.

Vashti didn't even try to continue working through the day. Pleading a migraine, something she had never had in her life and the mention of which drew a raised eyebrow from Ross Chandler, along with an unexpected acceptance, she left the office. She had no destination, no conscious desire to either go home, or anywhere else; she simply meandered her way through the downtown area, noticing nothing, seeing no one except as an obstacle to be avoided.

Images scampered through her mind as she walked, but they had no voices, made no sound. All they did was hurt, stabbing like knives, thudding like bludgeons. She didn't even notice when she finally, unthinkingly, arrived at home and flung herself on to her bed.

It was there, her tears staining the pillow even as her fists beat and thumped at it, that she heard again the accusations, saw the raw triumph in Janice Gentry's eyes.

Later, time no longer relevant, she stripped off her rumpled clothing and stood under the shower until the hot water ran out, scrubbing and scrubbing as if soap alone could remove the injustice, the hurt.

She was back at work by mid-afternoon, still hurt, still angry, but under total control. None of her colleagues, she felt, could detect the fragility of that control, and it didn't matter anyway.

CHAPTER FIVE

THE flowers arrived at four forty-five. Two dozen roses, all red.

It was such a surprise that Vashti had accepted the box and was watching the delivery girl walk away before she realised what was happening, what *had* happened.

She opened the box, then shut it again, wrinkling her nose as if she'd just smelled something rotten, laid it on her desk for a moment, then opened it again just enough to reach in and liberate the note that was tucked into the bouquet.

Without reading it, without even *looking* at it any more than absolutely necessary, she ripped it into small, then smaller pieces, and discarded those in her waste-basket. Then she went and washed her hands.

The girls in the general office downstairs thought the roses were lovely.

The letter arrived in the next morning's mail, and she had it half read before the contents became obvious. It was an apology from Janice Gentry—or what passed for an apology. Couched in the politest of terms, and brief to the point of ridiculousness, it was more insulting, Vashti thought, than apologetic.

What it really said, she thought, was, I'm glad I said what I did and I'm glad it hurt. This apology is only because *he* insisted I make it.

That, too, was ripped into infinitesimal pieces and consigned to the waste-basket, followed by its envelope.

Vashti's next step was to instruct the switchboard that she was involved in some critical work and absolutely *must* have as few interruptions as possible. And she *must* have the identity of any caller *before* she would accept the call. The roses paid for themselves twice over, there. She was, for the moment, quite popular downstairs.

By the end of the morning, having refused Phelan Keene's calls seven times, she could feel that popularity ebbing just slightly. That honeyed, chocolate-fudge voice was obviously working its wiles on the switchboard operators.

'I'm too busy to speak to him,' she instructed after returning from lunch to find notes of another *three* calls. 'I know what he wants and it isn't as important as he says it is, so for the rest of the day—for the rest of the *week*—just inform him I am not here.'

That got her through the rest of Tuesday. At work. At home it wasn't quite so simple; there was no obliging switchboard operator there to screen her calls. But there was, thank heaven, a telephone with a ringer that could be switched off, and, after hanging up on Phelan Keene for the second time in what seemed as many minutes, Vashti turned off the phone.

A few minutes later, having thought about it, she also turned out the lights, locked the door, and lay down on her bed in the dark. She'd had no dinner, but, with her stomach surging with the confusion of her emotions, wasn't sure she'd be able to keep anything down anyway. She finally drifted into a troubled slumber, only to wake shortly after midnight, hungry and no less troubled.

She felt a fool as she slunk through the flat, parting the lounge curtains ever so carefully so as to peer down on the street below, half certain she would see Phelan Keene's old utility crouched there, waiting, predatory as the man himself. She felt more of a fool when she found only the usual vehicles parked outside, yet couldn't quite summon the courage to turn on the lights and cook herself something to eat.

The refrigerator yielded three cheese slices and a carrot; her three remaining slices of bread were rock-hard and inedible, and she nearly scalded herself trying to pour boiling water into a coffee-cup in the dark. Not that it mattered; when she tried to drink the coffee she found she'd put in two spoons of coffee and one of sugar instead of the other way round, and had to pour it out and start over.

'This is idiocy,' she muttered, tiptoeing into the bedroom to stare at the clock's one-fifteen a.m. message. Then she stomped back to the kitchen, drank half the coffee before tossing away the other half in disgust, and returned to bed.

At first light she was busy making herself bacon and eggs and toast and jam and *proper* coffee, feeling even more a fool than she had the night before. Until she turned on the phone again and found it ringing almost immediately.

No prizes for guessing who it would be, she thought. At this hour? Nobody else that she knew would even be awake, much less have the nerve to ring anybody on the telephone.

'I won't answer it,' she said aloud. 'Damn you, Phelan Keene—I *won't*!'

And she didn't; instead she turned the ringer off and returned to a breakfast that had suddenly become inedible. She dressed, *drove* to the office, and within five minutes had organised herself a trip to Triabunna for the final tidying-up of an earlier job. There wasn't all that much to be done, but it would keep her out of the office and away from the telephone, she thought. Forgetting, until it was too late, that driving provided her with far too much time to think, when thinking was just what she wanted to avoid.

As she wound her way towards the coast, forced to concentrate on her driving by the constant presence of log trucks that loomed up behind her with fearsome determination when loaded and swayed alarmingly when approaching empty and headed back inland, she found the incident and all its ramifications flouncing through her mind like the aftermath of a pillow-fight.

Janice Gentry's involvement was the easiest to comprehend and—surprisingly—to simply ignore. It was nothing more or less than sheer bitchiness, so obvious a ploy that she ought to have expected it.

But the accountant's use of such a ploy in Phelan Keene's presence suggested, at the very least, that it was a subject she had already discussed with him. And if with Phelan, then logically also with his brother and sister. But when?

Surely, Vashti thought, it couldn't have been *before* the weekend; it was ludicrous, considering Alana Keene's warm and genuine attitude on Saturday, to assume Alana could even have been aware, at the time, of Janice Gentry's vindictive accusations.

Sunday? Possible, she thought. Probable, she ultimately decided, reviewing in her mind all that had happened. Phelan had obviously intended to see the Gentry woman on Saturday evening, probably *had* done so on Sunday.

Was the accusation linked to his earliest meeting with Vashti, when he'd been undeniably hostile, and quite clearly marked her as 'the enemy' and treated her as such?

That, she thought, made some modicum of sense, but only if she could ignore Saturday entirely. Surely no man could be so...so attentive, so charming, to a person he thought guilty of such behaviour?

It was *that*, she decided, that galled the most. Such behaviour was not only unthinkable to her personally, given her regard for old Bede Keene—it was damned well unprofessional!

And for him to have spent half of Saturday being deliberately nice to her, *more* than just nice. To have used his charm so blatantly, to have touched her, kissed her...when he felt like that. It was disgusting!

All these thoughts dashed helter-skelter through her mind as she drove mechanically, avoiding the log trucks, back to Hobart that afternoon, arriving at the office just at knock-off time.

She skimmed through the various telephone messages, mostly from Phelan Keene and automatically, therefore, discarded unread, than locked up her desk again and drove home.

She had parked and was halfway up the footpath when the decrepit old utility clanked to a halt behind her small sedan, and, although she did her best, Vashti couldn't reach her door and get herself safely behind it before Phelan Keene's strong fingers were clamped firmly around her wrist.

'Let go of me.' She growled the command without looking at him, twisting her body in a futile attempt to enforce her demand.

'Not a chance,' was the reply, soft and yet threatening in her ear. Long, tanned fingers reached out to pluck her keys from fingers too weak to resist, and he reached forward to unlock her apartment door while still holding her in an iron grip.

'In!' he commanded, his voice overriding her own squeal of protest. And in she went, thrust into her own home like a bag of groceries.

Vashti stumbled forward, almost tripping over her own coffee-table as Phelan slammed the door behind them. Even as she regained her balance and turned to cry out her objections to this invasion, he was flipping on the night-latch and turning to face her, eyes blazing.

'Now,' he said. 'No telephones, no lying little switchboard operators, no screaming hysterics.'

Vashti could have laughed at the last; her breath was coming in uneven gasps, her heart was thumping as if to batter its way out of her breast, and she thought her legs would collapse beneath her any instant.

'Get out. Leave me alone,' she gasped. 'Get out... get out...get out...'

'Not,' he said grimly, 'until we've talked this thing through.'

'There's nothing to talk about,' she snapped in reply, part-way back in control now. 'Nothing!'

'The hell there isn't.' And his voice was as fierce as her own was angry, the fierceness matched by the explosive expression in his ice-green eyes.

'There isn't.'

He was dressed as her mind always pictured him now, in faded jeans and a light checked shirt with the sleeves rolled up to reveal his powerful forearms. His hair was its usual curly crispness and, although he was clean-shaven and smelled of the unique aftershave he used, his face was drawn, the shadows under his eyes revealing . . . what?

Certainly they weren't revealing anything like a quiet, even temperament. He stalked towards her across the tiny battleground of her lounge, looming huge in the small room. Vashti backed away the few steps available to her, then squealed with alarm as he reached out one forefinger and quite literally *pushed* her backwards on to the sofa.

'Now listen,' he growled, shaking that same finger in admonishment, as if by the very action he could forestall any attempt to argue. He kicked aside Vashti's handbag, which she'd dropped as he pushed her, and stepped closer, so close that he had to bend to look directly into her eyes.

'No!' She shook her head, lifting both hands to cover her ears, knowing it appeared childish—probably, in fact, quite ridiculous—but doing it anyway. Just to be doing *something*, anything but just accepting his assault.

'Yes!'

He reached down and lifted her by the wrists, forcing her nose to nose with him, glaring into her eyes and shaking her so vigorously that it seemed her arms would be wrenched from their sockets.

'I had no idea Janice Gentry was going to say what she did.'

He made the statement in direct, forceful tones, keeping his voice flat, almost totally unemotional.

'Who . . . cares?'

Vashti's voice was far from flat; the two words burst from her gasping lips, pushed by the pain in her shoulders as much as by the emotional pain she felt and tried to disguise.

'I care. And you care, whether you want to admit it or not,' was the reply, not flat now, but growled from lips only inches from her own.

'I don't. Let me go! Damn you, let me go, I said.'

She might as well talk to the wall. His fingers never slackened for an instant, nor did he ease his grip to let her get where she wanted most to be—away from him. No breathing space, no thinking space.

She didn't have to think; the thrust of her knee was almost instinctive. And, considering her position, should have been effective as well. Only he turned his thigh, or twisted his body somehow; she didn't know just what, only that instead of the release she expected she gained only a grunt of effort, a quick shake of his head as he negated her assault.

'Naughty,' he growled then. 'Not at all nice.'

Vashti lashed out again, knowing it was a waste of time but unwilling to give in.

'Stop that, dammit!'

'Let me go.' She gasped out the command, but tried to level her voice into a firm insistence, rather than the panicky response she felt inside.

'Not likely,' was the response, and his fingers clenched briefly round her wrists as if to accentuate the remark.

Vashti lapsed into what she hoped would seem passive acceptance, then lashed out in a third attempt to destroy his manhood, both feet kicking now, both knees thrusting, and felt a sudden great surge of joy as one toe struck something firm and she felt him wince.

Then, without warning, she was lifted, tipped half upside-down, and found herself sprawled in his lap as he landed with a thump on the sofa. One hand miraculously maintained the grip of two on her wrists while the other casually removed her shoes and then clamped itself around her knees, locking her into a totally helpless position.

'Right,' he growled. 'Now about all you can do is go for the jugular, and, although I wouldn't put it past you, I'll take the chance that the taste of blood would put you off. So I shall talk, and you, Msssss Sinclair, will listen. OK?'

With her arms stretched above her head and the rest of her body firmly controlled by his strength, Vashti didn't bother to reply. Instead, she glared up at him, baring her teeth and curling her lip in a snarl. Irreverently, she had a mental picture of a farm kelpie she'd once seen edging up to a fight, its teeth fairly clattering as it threatened. In any other circumstance, it might have been funny, but she now thought she knew how the dog had felt.

'I *did not know* that woman was going to say what she did,' Phelan said, spacing each word out as if he were someone predicting the end of the world. 'If I *had* known, I wouldn't have allowed it. Is... that...clear?'

His eyes burned into hers, then, unccountably, broke the contact to move slowly, deliberately, across her face, down her throat, and along the cleft of her dishevelled blouse. Vashti squirmed, which only made her more aware of the heat of his groin against her hip, of the way her skirt was rucked up almost to her waist.

'I...don't...care,' she replied, spacing the words as deliberately as he had. It was a lie, but he'd never know that, she vowed. Sort of a lie. What she *did* care about, suddenly realised was *all* she cared about, was whether Phelan Keene had believed the accusation. Whether he'd have allowed it didn't matter a damn; whether he *believed* it . . .

'Of course you care; stop being so obtuse,' he snapped. 'You're not a fool and we both know it, so quit acting like one.'

The comment was punctuated by a slow, circling motion of his thumb against the back of her knee, a motion so light in its touch that for an instant she wasn't aware of it. Then she was!

'Damn you . . . Stop that!' Vashti snapped, wriggling to no real effect against the strength of his grip. He did stop, too, which served only to make her *more* aware of the warmth where their bodies touched, of the male strength of him growing now against her hip.

'Stop what?' And his face suddenly changed, sliding into a picture of such bland, total innocence that she almost laughed. Again that insidious thumb, moving against the thin, delicate skin behind her knee, moving in slow, deliberate circles as his elbow kept her from kicking free.

Vashti didn't answer; she just forced herself to meet his eyes, to deny the effect he was having on her, to maintain her rage, her sense of betrayal.

One dark eyebrow lifted in a sarcastic query; his teeth flashed in a sudden, wolfish grin that disappeared as quickly as it began. And always his eyes, those pale, pale eyes, maintained their grip on her. He was so close that she could see the tiny rays of colour up through his irises, minute rays of cold that shot like sunshine through the green ice.

'This?'

His voice was a whisper of warmth against her lips, but the question was for a firmer touch, the warmth that went with the exploration of his fingers along the length of her thigh.

Vashti could answer neither, because as she parted her lips to speak they were captured immediately by his mouth. And as she writhed against the arousing touch of his fingers, the movement only served to make their journey more erotic, more intimate.

More maddening!

'Damn you,' she muttered, wrenching her mouth from his, shaking her head furiously to avoid a continuation of his kiss. 'Damn you...'

The curse was muffled this time, because as she stopped shaking her head to speak his lips were there to claim her, to stifle her curse half-uttered as his tongue tasted her breath, fluttered against her fury. And his fingers never stopped their caressing exploration, moving always closer to an objective that would defeat her entirely.

'You don't want to damn me,' he whispered after an eternity.

'I do...I do...' she sighed, lying to both of them now in the last vestiges of her defence. His lips remained only a touch away from her own; his eyes were huge, encapsulating her vision.

'Pretty hard to damn someone with your glasses all skew-whiff,' he muttered, and, miraculously, freed her legs as he automatically reached up to push them into place. It was a gesture she had, Vashti realised, already come to think of as 'special', as something somehow intimate between them.

Something he probably did to Janice Gentry's glasses as well, she now thought with a driving, hurting anger. And before he could reposition that hand she was twisting, thrusting, driving her body into a furious bid for freedom.

Waste!

He laughed, a laugh that seemed to boom through the small flat, as he twisted his own position so that he could clamp her legs between his own now, holding her even more securely than before.

But this left him with one hand free, free to explore her body at his leisure, ignoring her attempts to twist free, ignoring her objections, by the simple expediency of closing her mouth with his own, easier now that he had that free hand to manipulate her as he pleased.

His fingers touched at her jawline, gently but firmly shifting her head to make her mouth more accessible. And as he kissed her, that hand traced its deliberate way down the length of her throat, pausing only briefly at the hollow where her breathing bubbled with a curious mixture of fear and anger and passion.

Then he stopped kissing her, just for an instant, and his hand lifted to take her glasses away, lifting them from her nose as gently as his lips returned to claim her mouth.

Vashti was silent during that interval, silent and still as the proverbial church mouse. Her glasses gone, she somehow felt suddenly more vulnerable—given that could be possible—than before. And again, it divided her attention, as she instinctively worried about the spectacles, and, instead of avoiding his touch, was concentrating on what he would do with them.

And through her head, ridiculous at such a moment, ran the hoary old saying: 'Men seldom make passes at girls who wear glasses.' Over and over and over, like white noise, blanking out both anger and the warmth that now spread along her thighs, rising like mercury in a thermometer from where his erect maleness thrust against her.

'Not to worry.'

Had he actually said that? she wondered, unsure despite seeing his hand reach back to place the glasses safely on a side-table, *feeling* the hand return to lift the hem of her skirt, *feeling* the fingers trace intricate intimacies along her thighs.

Now his eyes followed, and their gaze as her skirt rode high, exposing all of her hips and thighs, increased her vulnerability as she felt her body temperature soar in response to his visual caresses.

'Stop.'

Her voice sounded false in her own ears, and sounded so weak that she wasn't sure he'd even hear her, much less pay any attention.

'But we haven't hardly begun.'

His voice was a delicate whisper now against her throat, a whisper translated as if into Braille by fingers that followed his words, down into the cleft of her breasts, touching just ahead of his breath, his tongue, his kisses.

The buttons of her blouse, miraculously having survived the writhing and twisting of her futile defence, now fell to his gentler, yet more insistent assault. And his lips followed to let his tongue touch at the edges of her bra, to the soft hollow between her breasts.

Vashti felt her breath go ragged; her nipples throbbed against the fabric of the bra until his fingers dipped to free first one breast, then the other, to his touch, to his mouth.

Her mouth parted in an agony of sensual torment; she could only writhe in helplessness as his lips fluttered against the warm softness, plucked at her nipples, and teased them to a magic life of their own.

Vashti could only sigh her delight, moan her acceptance; their argument, her earlier fury, both were barely memories now, memories from a past that grew more distant with each touch of his lips, each probing lick of his tongue.

Part of her yearned for him to free her hands, to let her return his caresses, allow her the freedom to touch his mouth, his hair, his muscular shoulders. Her legs, trapped as they were, yearned to be free, to be able to shift and allow his touch greater access to the secrets of her body.

And within her, the tiny voice of logic, of reason, of *danger*, screamed almost silently against the winds of her passion, the roaring of her blood, as it surged to meet his touch, to carry the messages of his fingers, of his lips.

'This is madness.'

The voice plucked at her conscience, at first timidly, then with growing force as she realised it wasn't her own voice, but *his*!

And even as her fevered brain cried out for an explanation, ignoring the body that screamed only for more of his kisses, more of his caresses, his lips fled from her nipples, his fingers lifted from their journey up her thighs.

'It's no way to have a discussion,' he said, reaching up now to touch her cheek, to seek her gaze with eyes somehow soft and gentle beyond all logic. Vashti met his eyes blankly, her own unfocused grey eyes those of a zombie, a sleep-walker. His voice crept into her consciousness, but the words held almost no meaning, made almost no sense.

Until, 'Are you ready to stop fighting me now? Ready to listen without trying to unman me or scratch out my eyes?'

That question got through to her, if only enough to make her cognisant of Phelan's next words, which he uttered almost dreamily as he reached down to tug her skirt down against the place where his own leg still held her captive. 'Sometimes I really do feel it's a shame they invented these damned tights,' he muttered, and the words were, she thought, more for himself than for her. 'Proper stockings are just so much...'

She could hear the rest without him saying it, could *feel* what he meant, could feel his fingers against the heat of her near-submission without the scanty protection of tights.

And for whatever reason—Vashti was no more capable of considering reason than she was of flying, given the situation—his words touched her mind like a torch to a still, unseen pool of petrol.

'You rotten mongrel,' she squealed, angered that he could have so assaulted her senses while still *himself* having the control to think about their original argument, their *business* dealings, while *she* had become lost—almost irretrievably lost—in the mingling of their feelings. *Her* feelings! Which made her all the more angry.

'I'll give you *proper* stockings,' she raged, and somehow this time *did* manage to writhe free of his grip, sliding between his legs to land with a thump on the floor, leaving her poised with her cheek against the firm heat of his groin, her arms clasped instinctively around his thighs as she fought for balance.

One of Phelan's hands reached down to grasp her elbow, lifting her towards her feet, but Vashti's own flailing arm struck it away as she lurched back from him, somehow caught herself upright, and stood glaring down.

How could he *be* so damned calm? How could he sit there, eyes placid, lips quirked into what she could only see—her missing glasses making a difference even at that short distance—as a self-satisfied smirk?

'Get out!'

Even as she snapped the command her fingers were busy tucking herself back into her clothes, all too aware of the sensitivity of her nipples as she bent to thrust her heaving breasts back into the spurious safety of her bra, even more aware of how clumsy her fingers were in trying to button up her blouse, twist her skirt into place, while fumbling to tuck in the sheer fabric of the blouse at the same time.

Phelan met her accusing, furious eyes with such calm self-assurance that it made Vashti more infuriated than ever.

'All that and we're right back where we started?' he asked, voice soft, unchallenging, yet somehow so arrogant, so damned *smug*, that she could have screamed.

'We're *nowhere*!' she shouted. 'Nowhere; do you hear me? We never were anywhere and we are never going to be anywhere. Now get out!'

'We came very close indeed to being *everywhere*,' he replied with a pointed hitch of one eyebrow. 'You might just think about that before you go all *thing* and start screaming and shouting and carrying on like a pork chop.'

'I've every right to carry on however I like,' she cried. 'It's *my* home, after all. You've got damned cheek, talking about having a *discussion*! You're an animal!'

'We all are, at least by some theories,' he replied calmly. 'Some of us are just better-looking than others. You, for instance. I'm not surprised we never seem able to have a rational discussion, when it drives me half crazy just looking at you.'

'You're more than half crazy,' Vashti replied without thinking. 'And my looks have nothing to do with it.'

'And if they have, they shouldn't,' he agreed amicably. 'Except to a male chauvinist piglet like me, of course. Not that I've ever denied being one; you'd only have to read one of my books to know better.'

Vashti could only stand there, staring down at him and trying to maintain her rage against this curious turn of the conversation. What on earth was he on about now? she wondered.

'Please go and sit down—over there where you're well and truly out of reach,' he said then, almost wearily, she thought. 'I shall promise to at least try and keep my hands off you if you promise in turn to stop fighting me, stop trying to put your own interpretations on every single word I say, and just *listen*! OK?'

Vashti continued to stand over him, her mind racing in ridiculous circles, starting and going nowhere, until she finally managed to force a stop to the process.

'I want coffee,' she then said decisively, and turned away, without waiting for any reply, to pad silently across the carpet and on to the chill tiles of the kitchen floor.

Phelan sat silent, elbows resting on his knees and his chin resting in his cradled palms as he watched her boil the jug, measure the instant coffee, get the sugar, the milk. He was still in that identical position when she finally set a cup before him and moved over to sit opposite with her own coffee, silent herself and, now, expectant.

Their mutual silence wafted through the room with the aroma of the coffee, but although Vashti watched the tall, pale-eyed intruder he seemed lost in introspection. He looked across the room without really looking; his eyes weren't focused on her, on the wall behind her, on anything at all that she could determine.

He sipped at his coffee without a word, without looking down at the cup, without looking across at Vashti. Lost in his own mind, she thought, and wondered without being all that surprised.

'I had a book half done when I flew down here for the funeral and all,' he suddenly said, still not looking at her. 'It's still half done. Not a single, solitary page further along than on the day I arrived. Haven't been able to think straight, haven't been able to concentrate. Just sit and stare at the computer as if it was some strange machine I've never seen before.'

Now he looked at her, or appeared to. And the expression in his eyes was one Vashti had never seen before—totally unreadable, totally obscure, and yet somehow pleading.

'Part of it's this damned tax business, for sure,' he continued. 'The old man's been driving me mad; he's driven us *all* mad now that he's gone and can't ex-

plain what he was doing or how or why or... or
whatever. I don't understand it, and neither does
Bevan or Alana—and they were *here* while it was going
on. I could only work from telephone conversations
I had with him there towards the end, and some of
that doesn't make a lot of sense even now.'

Vashti sat silent, her coffee forgotten as she listened, unable to make much sense out of what Phelan
said, but certain it was important she at least listen.

'What Janice said in your office the other day...'
he was very definitely focused now; his eyes held her,
forced her to listen '...was totally uncalled-for. And
if I'd had any idea she was going to take that track
in all of this, I would have...it would have...it
damned well wouldn't have been said!'

A fierce light blazed in his eyes as he made the
statement, then faded as Vashti sat silent, unsure what,
if anything, she ought to reply.

It shouldn't have been said? Of course it shouldn't
have been said. It shouldn't even have been thought,
much less said. But that wasn't the issue, and Phelan
Keene seemed incapable or unwilling to see what *was*
the issue—from her point of view.

Still silent, she rose and picked up both their coffee-
cups, then walked back to the kitchen to refill them.
There was, she decided, something to be said, something she *must* say, but she didn't have the faintest
idea what it was. Certainly it was *not* to comment on
how she could *feel* Phelan's eyes following her as she
moved, how she could tangibly feel their exploration
of her ankles, her calves, her hips. She had the
strangest urge to spin round, to confront him with her
knowledge, but she knew somehow that she would
never catch him out. If she turned, he would be

looking somewhere else, ostensibly innocent. Or, worse, he would be deliberately chauvinistic, not only letting her catch him, but planning for it, expecting it. She kept her attention on balancing the coffee-cups as she returned, not even trying to meet his eyes until she was seated again.

'I would be quite happy to turn this whole thing over to some other field auditor.'

The words were uttered even as she thought them, and only when it was too late did she realise her statement was less than totally honest. The examination of the old man's affairs was over and done with now, to all intents and purposes. But if she withdrew, even at this late stage, somebody might have to go right back to the beginning, creating more cost and more emotional turmoil for all concerned. *She* knew instinctively that the old man had been honest as the day was long, had made no deliberate attempt to evade tax. Just as she knew she hadn't harassed him into the grave because of it!

'What—so we can start all over again?' Phelan asked as if reading her thoughts. 'Waste of everybody's time.' And he picked up his second cup of coffee, lapsing into a silence that seemed to expand like smoke, filling the small flat, almost suffocating in its intensity.

'My car ought to be here on Friday,' he said then, not looking at Vashti, indeed looking at nothing in particular and making the statement as if to totally change the subject.

She nodded, but said nothing. Surely no comment was called for, she thought.

'And not before time, either. I'm getting awfully sick of driving that cranky old paddock ute the old man thought was so wonderful.'

Again, what to reply? She merely had another sip of her coffee and waited, until she was finally forced into some response simply by his silence.

'That's nice,' she replied. And wondered why she felt like a stray cat confronted by another stray cat, circling, cautious, ever ready to advance or retreat, ever ready to avoid any form of commitment until there was no choice left at all.

Now, she thought, might be the perfect time to be bold, to ask Phelan Keene straight out about this book he was writing, about this exposé of the tax office, about *her* role in all of this. Was he really, as he seemed to be implying, so taken with her that his writing was affected? The thought of his mooning about like a lovesick teenager was ludicrous, at best. Why couldn't she laugh? More likely, she thought, something she had said or done had put him off his original line of thinking. Was that it? Was she so different from his preconceptions that his entire script had come adrift?

Whatever, now was the time to ask. So why couldn't she utter the words that rolled around in her mouth like all black jelly beans, which she hated?

Because I...can't, she silently admitted. And hated herself for the cowardice.

'You're happy, then? It's finished now?'

His questions seemed innocuous enough; his voice showed no sign of aggression, no sign of anything, really. Vashti held off answering until she'd taken the time to listen—*really* listen, this time—to what he said and how he said it.

'I would certainly hope so,' she finally said, meeting his eyes, then looking away as she reached up to adjust glasses that weren't there and then cursed herelf for the mistake.

Phelan's generous mouth quirked just a bit as he reached to the side-table, picked up her glasses, and reared up out of the sofa to hand them across to her. The very movement was so swift, so wolfishly agile and quick, that Vashti found herself flinching away.

'Stop being so touchy; I've already proved that I can control myself,' he muttered, sitting back down as abruptly as he'd arisen. 'Not that I expect you to believe that.'

'I should certainly hope not,' she snapped, refusing to admit to either of them that it had, indeed, been *he* who had halted their encounter, not daring to admit to herself that she had been within seconds of total and absolute surrender.

'Do you really *need* those glasses?' he asked then, and, without waiting for a reply, 'Or do you just wear them as the business girl's first defence against roving male chauvinist pigs?'

'That's hardly worth bothering to answer.'

'Just as well; I think they're sexy as hell. They make your eyes look even bigger than they are,' he replied, leaning slightly towards her, his gaze snapping across the room like a lasso to capture her attention and hold it.

'Well, then, maybe you need glasses yourself,' Vashti replied, unaccountably flustered by the directness of the compliment, presuming it was intended to be a compliment at all!

'You wouldn't understand, but I'm inclined to agree with you,' was the curious reply. 'At any rate, I've said what I came to say, and——' with a mischievous grin '—perhaps just a bit more. What I'd like to know just now is whether you're going to accept it or not.'

'Accept what?' Vashti retorted. 'Being man-handled in my own home, being insulted, being——?'

'Accept that Janice's accusations weren't my idea and weren't made with my approval,' Phelan interrupted coldly. 'I don't mind if you can't or won't accept my apology; I just want the point made...that's all!'

'Consider it made.'

One dark eyebrow lifted in obvious scepticism, then lowered again, as did the temperature in the room, Vashti rather thought.

'Right,' he said, rising abruptly. 'I'll be off, then.' He had the door open and was halfway through it when he suddenly turned and said, 'And thanks for the coffee, by the way.' He was gone before she could reply.

Vashti sat there, staring at the now vacant doorway, only half aware of the sounds of the farm utility chugging to life, then rattling away down the street. Her mind whirled in a disjointed attempt to make sense of it all, to try and understand how Phelan Keene could be so damnably changeable, and, worse, so damnably capable of manipulating both her mind and her emotions until she hardly knew which end was up.

Eventually, none the wiser, she absently went through the routine of changing, cooking herself dinner and—far earlier than usual—showering and getting ready for bed.

As she stood under the soothing warmth of the shower, the encounter with Phelan replayed itself over and over in her mind.

As she soaped her breasts, it was to feel his touch, his lips so much warmer than the shower, so much more intimate than her own. It was as if her body had some unique memory bank of its own, one capable of endless memories of his kisses, of the ability his fingers had to rouse her, to lift her through layers of ecstasy, along paths of intimacy she could neither forget nor ignore.

If only, she thought as she drifted into sleep, she could somehow have met Phelan Keene without either of them being involved at a business level.

The thought remained with her through the night; it must have, she thought upon waking, to find it still on her mind. But with a new day came a more realistic outlook. Phelan Keene's involvement was, at best, purely physical, a simple matter of lust. At worst, he was deliberately manipulating her for his own advantage, or at least to *her* disadvantage.

A girl with any sense at all, she reasoned as she entered the office that morning, would march straight into the boss's office and have the entire Keene file transferred to somebody else—of course she would—but she didn't, for some reason or another.

A girl with any sense at all, she reasoned almost eight hours later, would not be idly browsing through the city's most exclusive hosiery salon, much less sending her bank card into orbit over shockingly expensive stockings and something astonishingly wispy and fragile to suspend them from.

CHAPTER SIX

THE exercise in extravagance seemed little short of ridiculous by Monday morning, and the morning's usual first exercise—reading the paper over coffee and a flaky croissant—did nothing to improve Vashti's sense of folly.

Once again the social pages affronted her with a photo of Phelan Keene being swarmed over by the sultry figure of Janice Gentry, this time wearing—what there was of it—something clinging, light-coloured and unquestionably expensive.

And slit so high along one—the photographic—side that the accountant's taste in frilly garter-belts left nothing to the imagination.

Phelan Keene, handsome in his own particularly understated fashion, seemed oblivious—or so Vashti thought from his expression—to the vivid display of feminine flesh that threatened to engulf him. Or was it, she wondered, her imagination? Certainly it wasn't important anyway.

Vashti used that section to wrap up the soggy, tasteless croissant. She was too busy to take time over the crossword puzzle on the next page anyway.

She took herself to dinner that evening at a new little restaurant about which she'd heard nothing but rave reviews, but didn't even bother to stay for dessert and coffee. This, she had decided by then, must be where her morning croissant had been made, probably by the head waiter doubling as an amateur pastrycook. How everybody else in the place could so obviously be enjoying their meal was beyond all logic.

Every morning that week, her impromptu extravagance of the previous Thursday looked accusingly at her from her lingerie drawer; on Friday morning she tucked the minute parcel under an old jumper in the bottom drawer of her bureau and kicked the drawer shut.

'Are you as cranky as you sound?'

The voice of Alana Keene, irrepressibly and annoyingly cheerful, fairly bubbled through the telephone a few hours later.

'Worse. Why?'

'Because I was going to buy you lunch, but if you're like that I might change my mind.'

'You probably should; I'm not fit company even for myself,' Vashti replied honestly.

'Gone off your tucker?' Nothing if not direct, Vashti thought. Living with those two brothers had probably given Alana an unbreakable vivacity.

'A bit,' she admitted, glancing down at the remains of an apple Danish, half eaten and discarded, like every other that week.

'Hah! I never would have guessed. And I don't suppose my dear brother has anything to do with this?'

'Certainly not!'

'Shall I bring him, too, then?'

Alana waited through the silence, then giggled at the success of her gambit. 'I couldn't anyway,' she finally said. 'He's out at Dad's...gone all broody, or hermity or something. Even crankier than you sound. Probably off *his* tucker, too.'

Vashti kept silence, refusing to rise twice to the same bait. Not that it did her much good.

'I reckon it's PMT, myself. Him, that is; not you. Anyway, I'll come get you at noon and we'll walk down to the Mona Lisa. Unless you want to go really up-market, in which case you can phone for a booking and we'll go to Dear Friends,' Alana suggested.

'How about the take-away on the corner?' Vashti countered. 'Even that's beyond my budget this week, but I'd stretch it that final inch, seeing it's you.'

'That bad, eh? Maybe I ought to send Phelan instead, and the two of you could sit opposite and just depress the hell out of each other.'

Alana again waited through the silence that followed, then conceded, 'OK, it was a silly thing to say, and I'm sorry. Meet me outside at noon; we'll go to the Mona Lisa and I promise I won't so much as mention the mongrel.'

Whereupon she hung up before Vashti could say no, only to ring back thirty seconds later to announce, 'I forgot to tell you that the reason I'm doing this is because I sort of need a favour. See you at noon.'

And when Vashti emerged from the building at noon, Alana was there, her normal bright smile like a banner that sagged visibly when they were close enough for her to see Vashti's haggard expression.

'Not only off your tucker, you haven't been sleeping real good either, I see,' she said with a shake of her auburn hair. 'If I were you, I think I'd take a sickie for the afternoon, have a long and very liquid lunch, and then try and sleep until Monday. But I suppose that would be asking too much, eh? Hardly professional.'

'Hardly,' Vashti agreed, not bothering to admit that she'd been thinking the exact same thing.

She knew her eyes were hollow, knew she was as tired as she looked, if not more so, and knew also that she was not about to be led into any discussion at all about why she looked and felt so weary.

It wasn't that she didn't feel Alana could be trusted; it was that both girls knew Phelan's sister was blatantly matchmaking, which was the absolute last thing Vashti needed just at the moment.

Neither did she need the minor effort of introducing her companion to Ross Chandler, but it couldn't be avoided when the boss emerged while they were still standing there.

Chandler acknowledged the introduction gracefully, his shrewd, tiny eyes glinting with appreciation of Alana's youthful loveliness.

'Make it a long lunch,' he suggested upon being told their plans. 'In fact why not make it an executive-type Friday lunch, Vashti? And I'll see you Monday— hopefully looking a bit more rested.'

'You must be some kind of witch,' Vashti said after the man had departed with a beaming smile at Alana. 'I've never seen him react like that to...well... anybody. I'd have bet I could have been dying on the floor in front of his desk and he wouldn't have given me the afternoon off.'

'Sex appeal,' Alana replied with a flashing grin. 'Does it every time; you ought to try it some time.'

Vashti didn't bother to reply, merely raised one eyebrow. Alana took the hint. They walked down to Liverpool Street and their restaurant and began a lengthy lunch in which Alana did her very best not to mention her brother.

Not that her best was all that good; it seemed to Vashti that every second comment had to be amended or cut short because it might involve some mention of Phelan, where he was or what he was doing.

And when Alana finally gave up and changed the subject entirely, things only got worse. Vashti herself became the centre of discussion and, as usual, Alana was less than tactful.

'I invited you for lunch because I've been worried about you, for some reason,' she said. 'And now that I've seen you, I'm glad I did. You look like something the cat dragged in at midnight, if you don't mind me saying so.'

'Thank you so very much; just what my ego really needed,' Vashti replied with a weary smile and a shake of her head. 'Have you got any other compliments, or is that your best?'

'Better than you deserve, love. What on God's green earth have you been doing to yourself? Or I suppose I should ask what Phelan's been ... oh, sorry.' And Alana had the good grace to at least try to look contrite.

Only to blow it all, in total innocence, a moment later by trying to change the subject and embarking on a dissertation involving stockings and suspender belts.

'Absolutely stunning,' she was saying, 'except for the price, of course. You just wouldn't believe what you've got to pay for...'

And halted mid-sentence in astonishment as Vashti's face contorted with spasms of laughter she fought to contain within, lest she explode into either tears or laughs that would make their table the centre of attention in the crowded restaurant.

'Put my foot in it again, eh?' Alana quipped without showing the slightest remorse. 'And of course you wouldn't dream of telling me why that was so hilarious.'

'I...I...can't,' Vashti gasped, hardly able to speak at all through the emotions that bubbled up inside her. And hugged herself, eyes downcast. If she tried to explain she'd either burst into tears or scream with laughter, and she didn't want either. Not here; not now.

Instead, she gulped down the remains of her drink, kept her eyes averted as Alana ordered refills for both of them, and struggled to assemble control—at least *some* control—before the waitress returned with the drinks.

'It's not your fault,' she said after the refill arrived and she'd finished half of that, too. 'It's just that, well, I went out last week and blew my plastic absolutely into orbit on exactly that. And I don't even know *why*!'

'Well, I do, of course,' Alana replied matter-of-factly. 'And no, I won't mention the mongrel's name.'

'Good. Don't.'

'I said I wouldn't and I won't,' Alana replied almost snappily, conveniently forgetting that she already had and didn't—in any event—need to do it again to keep the conversation in troubled waters. 'But if that steak doesn't get here pretty damned soon, I'll mention a few others.'

'Having told the nice lady we were in no hurry at all,' Vashti remarked. 'Now who's being cranky?'

'I always am when I'm hungry,' was the reply. 'Or when I start dumping grog into an empty stomach. There are people who really shouldn't drink, and I think I'm one of them.'

'Just makes me sleepy,' Vashti replied, but was as pleased as her companion when their steaks arrived a moment later.

'You get stuck into that,' Alana said, suiting action to her own words. 'It's hard to say from looking at you which you need more—the food or the rest.'

They finished up with rich desserts and coffee with liqueurs, by which time Vashti could hardly keep her eyes open. Alana, by comparison, had returned to her usual brightness and was carrying the conversation virtually on her own.

'Which is a waste,' she concluded. 'I can stay home and talk to walls at far less expense and you *should* be home, before you go to sleep where you're sitting. So I'll be quick about asking this favour and then we're going to put you in a cab and send you home.'

Presuming Vashti's nod to mean she still had an audience, she reached into her handbag and pulled out a small tan-coloured envelope, from which she finally extracted a theatre ticket.

'Presuming you've wakened up by tomorrow night, and presuming you wouldn't knock back a chance to see the Chrissie Parrott Dance Collective from the front row of the dress circle, and presuming you're even listening to me—are you?'

Vashti managed another nod.

'Right. So here's your ticket. I'm probably going to be late, so don't wait for me; just get there on time yourself and I'll make it when I make it. See here? It says eight-fifteen, which as you know means you'll have to be there a bit early, because the old Theatre Royal can be slow filling up.'

'But . . . who . . . why . . . ?'

'Because Ph...that mongrel who shall remain nameless was supposed to go with me and now he won't and I hate going alone, that's why. Now are you going to be in it or have I just wasted lunch and have to run around finding somebody else to join me?'

There was laughter in Alana's eyes, but a hint of something else, too. Maybe, Vashti thought, she really *did* hate going out alone.

'Thank you,' she said, reaching out for the ticket. 'For this and for lunch, which, no, was not wasted. I will join you, I promise, unless I somehow manage to sleep right through from the moment I get home today. And even *I* couldn't manage that, I don't think.'

'Good. Now let's go find you a cab. I'd drive you, although not after the liquid part of that lunch, except that I am without transportation until my *sane* brother, whose name I *can* mention, gets round to collecting me. Provided he remembers, of course. He may be saner than the other one, but he's a damned sight less reliable sometimes.'

It astonished Vashti when she wakened to find herself feeling so rested, so *totally* rested, and her bedroom still bright with daylight. Until she realised it was morning daylight, confirmed by the digital bedside clock-radio.

'Four in the afternoon until near as dammit eight o'clock in the morning,' she muttered aloud with considerable amazement. 'Well, I must have needed it.'

No lie there, and it would be something to tell Alana at the theatre that evening. On the way home in the taxi, she had wondered at the wisdom of accepting the ticket, had really not wanted to accept it in the first place. But this morning the idea seemed far more pleasant; she liked Alana and she liked modern dance and, well . . . why not?

Bouncing out of bed with a wondrous, unexpected feeling that, for once, all was right with her world, she climbed into her weekend housework clothes and rushed through the necessary chores—washing, ironing, even cleaning the oven.

Only then did she permit herself the usually earlier luxury of sprawling on the lounge floor to devour the weekend papers page by page, article by article. Two hours later she compounded the decadence by retiring to a hot, filled-to-the-brim bath with a jug of white wine and the latest novel.

Her buoyant mood persisted; when it came time to dress she had no difficulty making decisions. Out came the most flamboyant 'after five' outfit she owned. And with it, carrying a hint of apprehension small enough to be ignored, *the* lingerie.

'And to hell with you, Phelan Keene,' she muttered to a quite splendid image in the mirror. The stockings were, she decided, quite magnificent, and the fact that nobody was going to see what kept them up was irrelevant. *She* would know; she *did* know, and that slight nuance of naughtiness almost made it worth the price.

The overall effect called for at least one drink at the Theatre Royal Hotel before the show, so Vashti left with plenty of time in hand and was lucky enough to secure a parking spot just over the road from the theatre.

Outside the theatre, people were already gathering, dressed in everything from jeans to evening wear; Hobart was nothing if not tolerant about what should be worn to the theatre. Vashti strolled across Campbell Street at the first opportunity, nodding to several acquaintances, but searching in vain for Alana.

Even knowing her friend had expected to be late, Vashti kept an eye open as she moved into the throng at the pub next door and fought her way to the serving bar. Here, again, were one or two acquaintances, along with a fair few men whose glances said they'd like to be.

It was, she decided, quite worth the price of quality clothes to deliver so many sops to the ego in a single evening. Nobody made an out-and-out pass at her, which was just as well, thank you, but there was sufficient interest to make her brief stay in the pub exceptionally enjoyable.

Alana still hadn't put in an appearance, however, when the ushers began ringing their bells and it came time to find her seat. Vashti kept looking for her as she made her way across to the theatre, and, once inside, upstairs and along to the front row of the dress circle. Only two seats there were vacant, by this time, and she automatically settled into the one furthest from the central aisles, still looking round for her friend. But even when the lights had dimmed, then focused on the stage and the vivid intricacy of the first dance number, there was no sign of Alana.

The vacant seat was taken, however, during the first fade between numbers, and as the tall, lean figure of Phelan Keene politely made his way to her side Vashti felt herself grow first hot then icy-cold with anger at the deceptions that had to be involved.

She visibly shrank away from him as he levered himself into the seat beside her, saying nothing, not even looking at her. Nor did he, during the second presentation, which began almost the instant he was seated. He sat like a grim spectre, only his profile visible in the dim lighting, with his eyes and attention apparently focused on the lithe, almost hypnotic movements on-stage.

Vashti couldn't ignore his presence. Had she been blind and deaf, she thought, she would have known it was him the instant he sat down. But she could force herself to emulate his indifference, and she tried her best to fixate on the dancing, to try and let the musical accompaniment drown out the roaring inside her.

The music was good, the dancing better, the seats, unfortunately, still the most uncomfortable in the known world of theatre. But even as she sat with a self-constructed mental wall of thorns between herself and Phelan, Vashti was eventually able to give herself over to the performance and enjoy it.

Until the interval!

She had planned for it, hoping against hope that the people on her left side were smokers, and would move quickly to get out to the foyer. That way she could be free to leave without having to move through the tiny space before Phelan's legs, without having to look at him, to speak to him.

They did move quickly; he was quicker still. A hand caught her elbow before she had a hope of moving, and he was there, leaning to force her attention. So close, almost kissing-close, she thought irrelevantly. But kissing appeared the last thing on his mind.

He spoke. So did she, and their words were so much the same that it would have been laughable under any other circumstance. 'I'm going to kill your...my... sister for this!'

But it was Phelan who continued.

'You'll have to stand in line,' he said grimly, then grinned, his teeth gleaming but his eyes like coals. 'Unless you'd like to help, of course. This being the first thing we've ever agreed on, maybe we should share the experience.'

'*You'll* only kill her in a book,' Vashti heard herself reply. '*I* am going to...to...' Possibilities occurred to her—shocking possibilities—but she couldn't put them into words she was game to say aloud.

Especially as she had suddenly realised he'd let go of her elbow; now he held her wrist, and it was anything but a confining grip, the way his thumb moved caressingly across her pulse.

'Come and I'll buy you a drink. We can discuss the gory details after the performance,' he said, rising to his feet and lifting her along with him.

Never so much as a thought that she might not *want* a drink, Vashti thought as she toddled along behind him. Much less that she might not want a drink with *him*. And if he'd given her half a chance she wouldn't have left her wrap there on the seat; she could have just walked out and left him!

'This is too good to waste by stomping off in a huff halfway through,' he said. Reading her mind again? 'So if you're planning that, tell me now, and I'll just fetch one glass of wine.'

This was all spoken with a straight face and eyes that danced with devilish laughter, daring her to make a scene, double-daring her to take up his offer and flee, much as they both knew she wanted to.

'*White* wine, please,' she replied, calmly and politely. 'Which I may very well dump down the front of you,' she added to his departing back, noting as she spoke how superbly the dinner suit fitted him, how easily he seemed to make his way through the throng at the bar.

And when he returned, casually carrying two glasses of wine in one hand while he used the other to fend his way through the crowd, she wondered how he could do that so easily and never take his eyes off her the whole time. Because he didn't. From the instant he'd made sufficient progress to be able to see her, his eyes roamed over the terrain of her body, climbing a breast here, descending a leg there.

Did he realise how much the stockings he appeared to be admiring had cost? she wondered. Not to mention the wispy suspender belt that now felt more fragile than *risqué*? For an instant, as she reached out to accept the glass from him, she had a ridiculous desire to ask him, to see if he thought the price justified. Vashti had to lower her head to hide the inner laugh that thought caused.

'I hope that chuckle was prompted by some suitable punishment for my almost departed sister,' Phelan said. And his own grin was far from humorous. It was wolfish, totally predatory, frightening.

But his eyes weren't. They met her own over the wine glass he raised in a mocking salute, then brushed across her face with a curious gentleness, touching her lips, her throat...

'What I'd like to do to her, well, there aren't suitable words to be used in public,' Vashti said, raising her own glass before gulping half the contents down in a futile bid to cool her sudden flush.

'I agree. It's a pity Dad didn't use his good old razor strap on my dear little sister while she was growing up!' Phelan said. 'It might've put her off pulling stunts like this one!'

Vashti replied, quietly and seriously, 'But really, I'm just astonished that she'd even think of doing a thing like this. It's just . . . just . . .'

'Totally in character. My darling baby sister is probably the world's greatest pure romantic. She's been trying to marry off both Bevan and me for years, although to be fair tonight's little performance was a bit off the wall even for her!'

'She's off her head, never mind being off the wall,' Vashti retorted.

Phelan laughed, a curt, low bark that offered only a glimpse of flashing teeth and no real sign of humour. But whatever he might have been going to say was cut off by the bells recalling them to their seats.

Vashti followed Phelan down the darkening aisle, and was all too conscious of his hand on her arm as he guided her along the row and into her seat. She was equally conscious that he didn't maintain his touch once she was in her seat and the house lights went down to announce the second performance.

Throughout the second half, he maintained his attention only on the stage and the dancers, while Vashti found her own attentions divided. She very much enjoyed the performance, but was also very much aware of the tall figure beside her, of the strong profile lurking in her side-vision and even, she fancied, of the man's very aura.

Because Phelan Keene did have an aura, she thought. Or perhaps it was easier described as a *presence*; the semantics weren't important. It was enough that she was strongly aware—too strongly, if anything—of the man beside her, despite his silence, despite his apparent attitude of ignoring her.

When the show was over, stimulating several well-deserved curtain calls, Vashti turned to bend down for her wrap, only to find it already in Phelan's hands. Without thinking, she turned to let him spread it over her shoulders, feeling the touch of his fingers on her bare skin as he did so, fancying that his fingertips lingered briefly, tantalising. Or was it only fancy? Certainly it was fact that he took her arm to guide her into the aisle, that he kept her elbow in the cup of his palm as they made their way downstairs and out on to the crowded footpath.

'Dare I suggest we adjourn to the casino for a drink while we scheme and plot a dastardly revenge on baby sister?' he asked. 'We can drop your car off on the way, unless you're set on maintaining your independence to the bitter end.'

'I'll see you at my place,' Vashti replied before she could change her mind, and skipped across the street to her car before he could move to accompany her.

'You're an idiot, girl,' she muttered as she drove home. 'You don't make a whit of sense; not even to yourself.' And then laughed. Did it matter? Did anything really matter? It was a nice night, she'd just enjoyed a splendid performance, and been invited for a drink at the Wrest Point casino. She was dressed for it, in the mood for it, and so indeed—why not?

The totally carefree atmosphere was less easy to maintain once she'd parked her own car and got out to find Phelan Keen waiting to hand her into his own—a magnificent Jaguar that reeked of luxury and comfort. As they drove through the city and south towards Sandy Bay and the casino, she found herself chattering almost non-stop, as if by noise alone she could eliminate the feeling of luxurious intimacy created by both man and automobile.

Keene drove with seemingly careless flair, yet on several occasions during the journey she noticed how he deftly slowed or switched lanes to avoid possible problems, how he was totally alert to the traffic around and ahead of him without appearing to be. Was he equally alert to her, to her jangled feelings, her forced spontaneity?

If so, he concealed it well, handing her out of the big car at Wrest Point having said hardly a word since they'd left her home, casually taking her arm for the walk through the parking lot, but touching her only with his fingertips. And his eyes.

Vashti wasn't so confused that she didn't notice the admiring glances she attracted as they strolled through the hotel's reception area, Phelan apparently seeking a relatively quiet place where they could sit down with their drinks. He, too, attracted a degree of attention, she noticed, and wasn't a bit surprised.

He finally found a place for them, got Vashti seated and then said, 'White wine for you, *Mssss*, or something a bit more ... adventurous?' She shivered inwardly at the stretched-out Msssss, then noticed his eyes were laughing; he was only being cheeky, she hoped.

'Oh, definitely more adventurous,' she found herself replying. 'A piña colada, I think.'

'The perfect choice,' he replied. 'I shall return quite quickly, lest you succumb to the lecherous glances I see all round the room.'

Gone before she could even smile at his phoney pompous attitude, he was, indeed, back quite quickly with an enormous goblet for her and what seemed an innocuous glass of something colourless for himself.

'Now what shall we drink to?' he mused as he handed over her drink. 'I'd say revenge, but that's far too general, much too simplistic. There really ought to be a twenty-dollar word that fits, don't you think?'

'You're the wordsmith,' Vashti replied, her mind blank, empty now even of simplistic synonyms to take his meaning.

Their glasses had yet to touch, and he was holding her glance over the rim of his, somehow making the toast frivolous and serious at the same time.

'Well,' he said, '"vengeance" isn't bad, although I'm told it's the prerogative of the Bloke Upstairs. Some of our more primitive north-eastern neighbours call it "pe-bak"—in pidgin, of course. But that would mean all sorts of hard work, because we'd have to take her head and smoke it and shrink it, or eat her heart, or something equally gruesome. Too damned much trouble, say I. And "lex talionis", which is the Latin bit that requires punishment to fit the crime, wouldn't let us go quite that far, although I rather fancy the smoked head bit.'

'I just don't see myself as an avenging angel,' Vashti replied, smothering a grin and, still held by his pale eyes, suddenly dying of thirst, but unwilling to taste her drink without the formality of a toast. 'Couldn't we just let her off with a warning or something?'

'Not a chance!' And he clinked his glass firmly against hers. 'Here's to *retaliation*,' he said, stretching the syllables into, Vashti thought, a fifteen-dollar word, at least. But still . . .

'I'll drink to that,' she said dramatically. And did so, wishing she had the nerve to just come straight out and tell him that she was not, and would not be, a particularly vindictive person. Not, she supposed, that he would believe it anyway.

'And so you should,' he said with a grin that widened as he reached out with a napkin to dab ever so gently at the corner of her mouth. 'Froth in your moustache,' he said quite seriously. 'Should be more careful with frothy drinks.'

And laughed aloud at her instinctive gasp of surprise and the hand that flew to her mouth after his, leaving a curious feeling of intimacy, had gone.

Vashti could only laugh too then, but in her own ears it sounded false and contrived. Had she reacted too strongly? Certainly she'd been unprepared for such a gesture, was still having to force herself to be cautious with this man, to be *angry* with him, as she was supposed to be. But it was hard, indeed damned near impossible.

All he had done the other night, she was forced to admit, was make it very, very clear that he fancied her, that there was a strong sexual attraction. If she was going to deny vindictiveness, she could hardly lie even to herself about the fact that the attraction was mutual. But did she dare let herself relax?

'I know the classic line is something about you being so lovely when you're angry,' he said in that gentle, musing tone he sometimes used. 'But you're not. Or rather, you are, but it's nothing compared to how beautiful you are when you're not angry, when you're just being ... well, you.'

Vashti giggled; she couldn't help it.

'Thus sayeth the great communicator, the master wordsmith,' she chuckled, inordinately pleased at having, for once, caught him flat-footed. Then even more pleased, somehow, to have him join her in laughter. No super-ego here, she thought; a man who could cheerfully laugh at himself couldn't be all bad.

'I may have to take you on as a collaborator,' he said. 'Or, better yet, as a fair-dinkum research assistant.'

Vashti couldn't resist the opportunity.

'I thought you already had,' she countered. Then added, hoping against hope, 'Or have you given up this mad idea of writing a book centred around the tax department?'

'Not on your life!' he replied vigorously. 'There's a wonderful book there if I can just get a handle on it. And I will—all it takes is time. And of course the right approach. Which is where you'll find yourself more involved than you might imagine.'

'You want me to rush around in my spare time investigating the various aspects of murder, sex and general mayhem? In the staid, conservative old tax office?' Vashti chuckled, couldn't help it, really. The idea seemed quite ridiculous.

'No, not exactly that either,' he replied, and now she saw the devilment in his eyes. It was no longer relevant who had started this little game; Phelan was also starting to enjoy himself.

'The mystery and intrigue part, then? No good. I'm hopeless at mysteries; sometimes I don't even know whodunit after it's been explained to me.'

Silence, but silence with a shake of his head and one lifted eyebrow.

'Well, it can't be the steamy bits, because I'm...'
She had to pause, realising only too late how easily
he'd trapped her—or she'd trapped herself.

'Off the boil? I never would have guessed.'

And now the devil laughed in his eyes, eyes that
forced her to laugh with him, to accept, as he had,
the joke on herself.

'*Right* off the boil,' Vashti replied sternly after
granting him hardly more than a smile. He was too
tricky, too devious by half, she thought. And she decided to be far more careful with what she might say.

Phelan didn't seem the least concerned. He
shrugged off her stern message and gazed thoughtfully for a moment.

'OK,' he finally said, 'we'll let that one go for a bit
and look at the practicalities of the matter. Is this
evening tax-deductible?'

'I...' She paused, eyes narrowed as she glared at
him for bringing business into what had been a lovely
evening despite its unusual beginning. Then decided
to hell with it. 'I couldn't imagine how,' she declared.
'Everybody knows by now, surely, that entertainment
expenses are no longer allowed.'

'Well, please don't take this wrong, because I'm
only being hypothetical,' he said, 'but what if I'm not
just "entertaining" you? What if what I'm doing is
research?'

'Hypothetical research?' Vashti definitely, she decided, did not like the direction this was going. But
she couldn't see an easy way out; nothing short of
a blunt refusal to play the *hypothetical* game
would work.

'*Research* research,' Phelan insisted. 'Now try and be objective about this; we're only speculating, after all.'

'OK,' she replied, feeling no assurance whatsoever.

'Right.' Phelan was enjoying this; she could see the glint of battle in his eyes. 'Now you remember at lunch that day when I insisted that if I'm awake I'm working?'

'I do. Was that luncheon "*research*" too?'

'Don't be cheeky,' he growled. 'You know damned well it wasn't.'

'That doesn't prohibit your presuming *your* portion was research,' she replied astutely. And nearly laughed at the expression on his face as he thought about that and was forced to accept her point.

'OK, I could have. Let's say I did. But it's tonight—hypothetically!—that we're looking at. Surely it's a legitimate business activity for a writer to bring a girl to a place like this to *research* how she reacts to the place, how she dresses, how the bar service works, how the drinks look, how...well...everything? After all, I can't very well put it in a book if I've never seen it, now, can I?'

Vashti thought about his theory long and hard, so long that he finally grinned hugely, then got up and went off to get fresh drinks. When he returned, she was ready.

'But you've been here before,' she submitted. 'And you've been here with a woman before, I'm sure.' She faltered only slightly as a vision of Janice Gentry intruded. 'How many times do you expect the tax office to accept that as research?'

'I've never been here before with *you*.'

'What does that have to do with anything, for goodness' sake?'

'Well, if you're going to be my . . . let's say heroine, then it's *your* reactions that I'm researching, surely. Not somebody else's.'

'But I'm not your heroine,' she protested. Feebly, because this was getting all too complicated, therefore dangerous. Phelan didn't laugh, but his eyes were ready to. She was on shaky ground here, and didn't know where to step.

'Hypothetical, don't forget.'

'All right. Hypothetically, I'm your heroine. But I think you're really stretching this a bit. Surely any woman would do?'

'Certainly not! After all, if I'm doing a book in which *you* are the heroine, then I have to know how *you* react to everything. I already know how . . . how some other women react, but if you're going to be the heroine, then *you're* the person whose reactions I have to research.'

And every time he stressed the *you*, something flickered in his eyes, something that Vashti felt could actually reach out and touch her, caress her. Dangerous!

'So tonight I'm a hypothetical woman being researched as a hypothetical heroine,' she finally charged. 'What happens tomorrow night if you bring me here again? There has to be a limit somewhere.'

'I accept.'

'Well, I'm pleased; I didn't think you'd give in that easily,' Vashti replied, honestly surprised.

'Who said anything about giving in? I just said I accept your invitation for tomorrow night; that's all.'

'Now who's being silly?' she replied lightly, hoping to divert him, to defuse the trap before she was hopelessly snared.

And it worked!

'Tomorrow night,' he said quite seriously, 'I could bring you in, let's say, grotty clothes, or clothes that didn't fit, didn't suit you. Still the heroine, but I reckon the research element is still there.'

'And so on and so on,' Vashti mused, intrigued by his logic and ninety-nine per cent certain of how Ross Chandler would react to it. Then she thought about how close to the wind she might be sailing from a purely ethical basis.

'I think . . . I think we'd better let this go,' she said.

'A bit too close to home? Don't forget it's only hypothetical,' Phelan replied directly. 'And don't forget too that you, personally, are never going to have to find yourself having to deal with it professionally.'

'You're aiming to put me in a terribly compromising position, but it's all right because it's only hypothetical? Thank you so very much, I think.'

'I am indeed, and it's got nothing to do with taxes.'

He was only half joking, if that. His eyes told her that, his glance reaching out to stroke her cheek, to touch her lips, run a line of fire down her throat.

'I can't be a heroine and a tax auditor too,' she stressed, trying to hide her confusion.

'Ah, but that's where you're wrong,' he said. 'I've got it all worked out. What I'll do is a romance: female tax auditor—make that *beautiful* female tax auditor— gets all involved with the tax affairs of handsome, charming, debonair writer who has strange but firm ideas about how his tax should be assessed . . .'

He was looking at her quite strangely now, she thought, his words rocketing directionless through her mind.

'They could meet for the first time, let's say, in a remote little country cemetery, maybe, some place really dark and spooky and vivid with atmosphere. What do you reckon?'

Vashti didn't reply. She felt suddenly cold, as if someone had abruptly taken away all the heat in the room. She reached out for her glass, realising only then that it was once again empty.

'Another?' Phelan was on his feet, reaching out to take the glass from her. She nodded, still silent. He moved off into the crowd and Vashti unfolded her wrap and threw it over her shoulders.

What kind of game was he playing? For an instant, she found her mind clouded with stark terror. She was halfway to her feet, ready to run, before she managed to take a deep breath and regain control, or at least some semblance of control. By then it was too late to run.

'I don't think you fancy being my heroine, somehow,' Phelan was saying as he set her drink in front of her, then reached out to take her hand in his. 'And you're cold. Are you feeling all right?'

'Yes. Just . . . cold,' she replied. Worse than cold now. Freezing. Except that one hand, burning in his grasp as if both their hands were on fire.

Vashti felt like a mouse trapped by a cat. Not a hungry cat, which would at least perhaps ensure a quick and certain death. A cruel cat, a cat that would toy with its prey, tease, torment. Just, she thought, for the fun of it.

'Would you rather collaborate on retribution?' he was asking. 'You seemed to enjoy that more, I think.'

No, she wanted to shout. I don't want to collaborate on anything. I just want this to end. It was too dangerous, too risky by half—emotionally and ethically and personally and professionally.

She wasn't even aware of shaking her head, but she *was* aware of him lifting his eyes to look beyond her, of him suddenly releasing her hand, of his glance changing, evolving from what had seemed vaguely concerned to that tense, predatory alertness.

'Too late, I fancy. Best you gird up your lovely loins for battle, darling Vashti. And if you can't help, for God's sake don't get in the way.'

And before she could reply he was on his feet, grinning broadly, warmly, welcoming.

'Alana! Well, well. This is a surprise. Bit late for you to be out, isn't it, dear sister?'

CHAPTER SEVEN

VASHTI came to her feet so quickly, trying to turn at the same time, that she stumbled, saved only by Phelan's hand catching her arm, pulling her against him, and then reaching round to hold her that way.

Her eyes seemed out of focus for just that instant; she opened them to see Alana, dressed resplendently in the palest mauve, on the arm of a tall, strikingly attractive man about Vashti's own age.

Alana was open-mouthed, staring at her brother with the haunted, enormous eyes of a trapped animal. Poised to flee, but held by her unwitting companion, Alana seemed caught in a pool of silence; she stood there, eyes whipping back and forth from Phelan to Vashti, at first with pleading, then a sort of resigned acceptance.

Vashti couldn't speak. All her anger at the girl's deception had frothed up to lodge in her throat then dissipate as she emphathised with Alana's plight.

The freezing moment thawed, melted by Phelan's gentle voice as he smiled at his sister and reached a hand out to her companion. Introductions were made; Vashti forgot the young man's name as quickly as she heard it. It was, she knew, irrelevant in the face of the explosion to come.

Only it didn't. Phelan insisted Alana and her friend must join them for a drink, noted their preference, and walked off to leave the girls and Alana's unknowing companion. Vashti was numb, unsure of what to say, what to do. Alana, she fancied, was worse.

Someone's voice—Vashti realised after an instant that it was her own—chopped the silence into appropriate slices of small talk, forcing a response from Alana, coaxing one from her companion. Phelan was gone for minutes—hours, it seemed.

Then he was there, materialising from the crowd like a magician from a puff of smoke, an enigmatic smile on his lips and a tray of drinks on the cupped fingers of one hand. But his eyes! Alana's companion—what *was* his name?—had never met Phelan before, obviously. Or else he was just thick. Maybe both; surely nobody, Vashti thought, could miss the fire in those eyes, the explosive, wild madness.

Certainly Alana didn't. She accepted her drink, then sat there, staring at it as if it might leap up and take her by the throat. Occasionally she shot a look of pure panic at her brother, or at Vashti, who held on to her own glass as if to maintain her balance.

And Phelan dominated the situation. His rich voice purred like that of a hunting cat; his personality held all of them as if in a cage. Skilfully, using words like fencing foils, he drew out Alana's young man—who he was, what he did for a living, and did he ride? Of course, Alana wouldn't even *talk* to a man who didn't ride. Within minutes, it seemed, he knew more about the man than his mother did; Vashti still couldn't remember his name!

Then it was time for another round, and of course it was Alana's friend's turn to buy. He was gone for what seemed like days, *silent* days in which Phelan sat with a warm smile and ice-bleak eyes, pinning his sister in place, forestalling so much as a word from her by sheer will-power.

Alana seemed incapable of countering his silent assault, and Vashti was equally impotent. She wanted to cry out to Phelan, to somehow make him stop this torture, but it was as if she were locked out of the tableau, despite being a part of it.

Why didn't he say something? Why no accusation, no yelling or screaming or whatever it was that brothers and sisters did under such duress? Vashti merely wanted to get away, to go and hide under a table, if nothing else. The atmosphere was so alive with tension that she could hardly breathe; she was freezing and stifling at the same time.

Alana sat like a mannequin, so still that she didn't appear to breathe at all. Her eyes were wounded, her lips parted as if to gasp, or speak, or scream. Phelan smiled.

The boyfriend returned. Phelan turned the sound back on and conversation returned, but the tension remained—tangible, it seemed, to only three of the four.

Then Phelan began applying the pressure, *forcing* his sister to take an active role in the conversation, *making* her respond. He was truly a master manipulator, somehow engendering not only conversation but smiles, once even a laugh. Ghostly hollow, it was, but a laugh.

And he kept twisting the conversation, working it like potters' clay to find places for words like 'vengeance', 'vendetta', and a host of other synonyms. Each one seemed to strike his sister like a lash. Most had a similar effect on Vashti, but he couldn't realise that; seated beside him, she was on the periphery of his attention, she thought.

Wrong. He finished up with a line that allowed him to exhibit 'retaliation', then turned to favour Vashti with a smile so huge, so obviously genuine, that she couldn't believe it.

'Of course you're not a vengeful person, dear Vashti,' he grinned, but it was a false grin now. Then he rose to his feet and turned to his sister with an even broader, more false grin. 'Anyway, we have to go now,' he said to Alana, reaching out to her friend with an outstretched hand to be shaken.

Alana got a kiss on the cheek, then Phelan quietly said, 'You know...you've kept your figure really well. Must be all the riding. Give all the children a kiss for me when you get home, eh?'

And to Vashti, who simply didn't *believe* what she'd just heard, 'Come along, darling.'

Come along she must, because he had taken her wrist and was already turning away, leaving Alana standing there with a stunned expression and her companion looking like a man who'd just got his tax assessment.

Vashti would have been pulled along like the tail on a kite, except that as soon as they were out of the young couple's sight Phelan tugged her close to him and put his arm companionably around her waist. And the fingers there trembled, as did, she quickly realised, the hip she was being bounced against as they walked. A few steps more and he stopped, his entire body shaking.

The bastard was laughing! And so, despite the turmoil of emotion that threatened to blow her head off, was Vashti. Phelan turned her to face him, loomed over her with tears brightening his eyes as he chortled at the success of his gambit, and Vashti simply couldn't help but join in. They stood there, oblivious to the passing throng, and fairly howled with laughter.

'You were magnificent; the perfect foil,' he said after a minute, and leaned down to kiss her, almost chastely, on the lips.

'I wasn't being your damned foil,' she replied. 'I was just as dumbstruck by the whole performance as everybody else.' And somehow the humour had gone out of it, for her. 'You really are a cruel man,' she said bluntly.

'Fiddlesticks! The bloke was a nerd and she'll thank me in the morning,' he retorted. 'That's if she doesn't come blazing out to the farm and slaughter me in my bed. I don't suppose you'd let me stay with you to-night, where it's safe?'

Vashti ignored him. 'I really ought to go to her,' she mused. 'You had her absolutely terrified, you know? And that poor young man...'

'He probably won't figure it all out for a week,' Phelan replied. 'Stop fussing. When you've had a chance to think it all through, you'll realise it wasn't anywhere near as depraved as it sounded. Besides, it was *your* revenge too—or had you forgotten that?'

'I'm not a vengeful person,' she replied, throwing his words back at him, then suddenly aware that they were standing in the middle of the Wrest Point lobby, dividing the throngs of late-night gamblers and diners that flowed past them, and Phelan Keene was still holding her disturbingly close against him while he stared down into her eyes. One hand was acceptably enough placed on her hip, but the other...

'And all the prettier for it,' he replied, and for an instant she thought he was going to kiss her again. Vashti backed away the inch his hands would allow, only to have him whisper, 'And you've kept your figure well, too.'

Which brought an immediate vision of Alana's gentleman friend, rigid with astonishment. It was enough to break the spell that had been forming; Vashti couldn't stop herself smiling.

'It's the riding that does it,' she chuckled, and carefully kicked Phelan in the shin, just enough to make him release her. The gentle kick was rewarded with a grimace, but he *did* release her, only to take her arm immediately in a gentle but proprietorial grip.

'I don't know about you,' he said with a grin, 'but all this vengeance has me fair starving. Fancy a snack before we retire to plot some more?'

'No more! If I were your sister I'd shoot you for what you've done already,' Vashti cried. 'And no, I'm not hungry. Or rather, I'm not sure. I don't know whether to laugh—because it *was* funny, I suppose— or to be just as angry with you as your sister is.'

'If *I* were my sister, I'd be scampering for the nearest hills, rightfully fearful of more to come,' he replied grimly. 'That was just a taste of her own medicine; there's the rest of the bottle to come—and it's a big, big bottle that won't taste one bit good. I'm certainly glad that you're not my sister, by the way. It would make things very difficult indeed.' And his eyes made very clear what he meant by that; they literally devoured her. 'Do you gamble, by the way?'

'The way they do here? Hardly. I'm just a working girl, remember.'

'How could I forget? Actually, I'm not much of a punter either, just in case it worries you. But I do have my moments and tonight I feel rather specially lucky. Must be the company I keep. Let's take a stroll through the gaming rooms and see if you're as lucky for me as I'd expect.'

To which there was no rational answer, much less a safe one. Vashti allowed herself to be guided down to the glitz and glitter of the gaming rooms, thinking as they went that she must be out of her mind even *trying* to keep up with this man.

I am well and truly out of my league, she thought, only to compare that intellectual rationale with how pleasant she found Phelan's company, how much she actually enjoyed being with him.

Waiting while he exchanged money for chips, she idly glanced at the crowds which surrounded the various roulette and blackjack tables, their faces an education in itself. Most seemed to take their gambling seriously; it was the locals at the poker machines who radiated elation or dejection with each small win or loss. The serious gamblers didn't, she thought, seem to have much fun at all.

Phelan, she quickly discovered, could never be described as a serious gambler. Within ten minutes at a roulette table he quadrupled his stake, only to be down to a single chip five minutes later.

'A kiss for luck,' he said then, and plundered her mouth before she could even think to object. Taking the longest possible odds, his chip multiplied as if by magic into stacks and stacks that grew like mushrooms.

'You *are* lucky for me,' he said, removing his winings with a delighted grin. 'Now let's see how lucky you can be for yourself.'

'But I don't even know what's going on,' she protested. 'And I can't gamble with ... well, you know.'

'With my money? Course you can. You just take a chip like this——' and he put one in her hand, then guided it over the betting zone '—and put it where you fancy.' The chip dropped from nerveless fingers as he put his other arm around her, his touch moving gently at her waist, his hip against hers and his breath warm in her ear as he whispered instructions.

She lost. Lost again. And again. No third time lucky, nor fourth nor fifth nor sixth.

'This is crazy,' she said aloud, turning to Phelan, urging him. 'I've got to stop. I can't keep this up.'

'It's 'cause you've got no faith,' he smiled. 'Or maybe because I haven't kissed *you* for luck.'

It was a shortcoming he proceeded to rectify with a thoroughness that left Vashti gasping and flushed with a sudden shyness. She'd have been embarrassed beyond belief, except that nobody noticed! And it was time to bet, which she did with all she had left, at Phelan's insistence.

'You can't test kissing luck by being a piker,' he said.

'You only used one chip,' she protested, horrified at the thought of losing everything in one go.

'I only had one left,' he said with a shrug. 'And besides, I trusted you for luck.'

I don't have your faith, she was about to say. Only suddenly she did—because she won! The pile of chips was magically cloned over and over and over.

'I won!' she cried. And again. Her eyes were wide with delight, her breath coming in gasps of excitement.

'Again?' Phelan smiled indulgently, helped rake in her winnings—*their* winnings.

'Not on your life,' Vashti said. 'I'd have to be mad! There's nearly a week's salary there.'

Phelan reached out and retrieved a handful of chips. 'Minus our original stake. What's left here now is just play money; it doesn't matter if you win with it, lose it or burn it.'

'No,' she said firmly, raking in the remainder and pouring the chips into his dinner-jacket pocket before he could move to object. The gloss was gone now. The heady feeling of excitement had ebbed to become common sense. Or, at least, as much common sense as Vashti felt capable of in this man's presence.

Suddenly she was exhausted, sagging. And it must have been obvious, because he didn't argue, didn't protest, merely looked down into her eyes, his gaze warm and gentle and... sharing.

'Time I took you home,' he said quietly. 'You've had a busy day for a little girl.'

Ten minutes later they were again in his luxurious car, moving smoothly through the scant traffic along Sandy Bay Road. Vashti lounged against the leather of her seat, her mind coasting, revelling in the silence and the car's super-smooth ride.

When they reached her flat, Phelan walked her to the door, his fingers warm on her arm. She ought to ask him in, she thought, but tiredness combined with caution to hold back the invitation. If she'd been vulnerable the other night, tonight was doubly so, dangerously so.

And he seemed to know it, even expect it.

'I've enjoyed this evening very much,' he said, lifting her hand to press his lips against it, then, startling, to press a wad of paper into it.

'What?'

'Your share,' he said, voice very soft now. 'And don't spoil it by arguing. Use it to buy something sexy—not that you need it.'

'But I can't take this,' she protested, ignoring him, forcing the money back into his hand.

'You just did.' And he deftly reached out to tuck the wad down the front of her dress, his fingers tracing a seductive retreat after he'd done so, his eyes claiming her, his lips ready to forestall any further argument.

'We'll do this again some time,' he said, 'if my sister survives long enough to arrange it. Now take yourself to bed, because if I have to do it for you I'd end up putting all my good luck at risk. Goodnight.'

And he left her, leaving the warmth of his lips against her throat, the feel of his fingers along her breast, along the length of her back. Warm feelings ... right feelings. But ...

Vashti stood in the doorway as he walked back to his car, knowing she wanted to call out to him, to invite him inside, despite the certainty of what that would mean. Knowing exactly what it would mean, and hating herself for not having the nerve to find out.

'No guts,' she told herself as he slid into the big car, closing the door with an over-casual wave in her direction. Vashti stepped into the flat, resisting the temptation to slam the door behind her, to display her temper and frustration in some physical, angry gesture.

'No guts,' she said again, flinging her wrap to land on the sofa, flinging her purse to join it, and kicking off her shoes to let them sleep where they landed.

The dress she hung up. Even childish temper tantrums had their limits, she told herself. And the frothy-frilly underwear, the ever so sexy stockings and minuscule suspender belt that had promised so much and delivered so little went into the laundry hamper to live with fair-dinkum working clothes until next wash-day.

Phelan's money she flung on her dressing-table, then retrieved it and carefully tucked it beneath the old sweater in her drawer. Then she retrieved the lingerie and tenderly tucked that away too.

'Not your fault,' she found herself muttering, and ended the performance by flinging *herself* into a bed that somehow seemed too big, too... something. She tried to take herself into sleep with thoughts of even sexier lingerie, of Phelan Keene's response to it. Of how she *thought* he'd respond to it, of how she wanted him to respond.

Why hadn't he? He surely would have sensed her readiness, her wanting him. And, she thought, he'd have sensed just as thoroughly how tired she was... had been! Angry now and wide awake, she walked naked through her flat, picking up the shoes and putting them away, carefully folding the evening wrap.

Then she discovered she was hungry. *His* fault; if he hadn't mentioned it, she wouldn't be. She made herself a sandwich, forced herself to eat it; heated some milk, forced herself to drink it. Went back to bed, got up again, made some more warm milk, and took a long shower that became a short one when she found herself scrubbing her body and hating it, not wanting to see it, not wanting to touch it. Wanting *him* to touch it.

She finally tumbled into sleep through sheer exhaustion, her body driven to it despite the confusion in her head, only to find herself waking with the sun and the alarm clock she must have set without thinking about it.

'No...no...nooo,' she groaned, turning off the alarm and plunging back into the safety of sleep, only to be wakened five seconds later, it seemed, by the telephone.

'I'm going to apologise to you,' said a familiar voice. 'Because *you* deserve an apology. For everything. Especially for involving you with him. *Him*, I'm going to kill. Slowly.'

'Alana? Is this really necessary at this ungodly hour of the morning?'

'It's one o'clock in the afternoon. I've been wanting to ring since...well, since very early. *He* won't answer his phone, or has it turned off, or isn't there at all.'

There was a long pause while the implications, Vashti thought, rattled round like peas in Alana's questionable brain.

'Oh. Oh...oh! He's not...not there, not there with you? I never thought of that. Oh, dear.'

'You never thought at all,' Vashti replied, trying to keep her voice firm, but failing. The younger girl's confusion had brought back memories of the night before, and with them the giggles. There was no sense trying to be stern; already she could feel herself wanting to laugh. Then had a better idea.

'Would you like to speak to him?'

She listened to the silence, then rushed into it, suddenly alive with the idiocy of it all. 'I'll have to wake him; he's had a rather hard night of it, poor love. How are the children, by the way? You did give them all a kiss, I hope. Ah, there's the handle bit; he'll wake up now, I reckon...'

An explosion of laughter cut her off, then both girls dissolved into laughter together. But it was Alana who recovered first.

'Full marks for that,' she gasped. 'And I deserved it. Deserved last night, too, I have to admit. Damn Phelan! That's the first time ever he's caught me that flustered that I couldn't even defend myself. I've never *been* so embarrassed.'

'You deserved all of it, and more,' Vashti replied. 'As he'd tell you himself if he were here, which of course he isn't. You're damned lucky either one of us is speaking to you, or ever will again.'

'You didn't enjoy yourself? You must have, or you wouldn't have ended up at the casino with him, would you?'

'That,' Vashti replied hotly, 'is not the point.'

'Course it is.' Alana seemed suddenly totally recovered from her apology mode. And that, for whatever reasons, served only to make Vashti angry about the whole situation. She really hadn't been, before. She'd been too involved, she realised, in Phelan Keene—just as Alana had intended! Which now made her even more angry.

'It's not! The point is that you've been messing round with other people's lives like... like some damned teenager. Which you're not, although nobody could ever tell, the way you act sometimes.'

Silence.

'Well?'

'I said I was sorry.'

'Not good enough.'

'Didn't you even enjoy the dancing? It should have been wonderful, what it cost me for the tickets.'

'I'm surprised you don't expect me to pay you back.'

Silence.

Cruel, that. Vashti felt the first flutterings of unease. Perhaps, she thought, she was making too much of this entirely. Except that she was still angry!

'You probably should; you'll thank me for this one day.'

'Well, if that ever happens, which I doubt, I will indeed pay you for the tickets,' she snapped, only to find that remark the final flurry of her anger. She wanted to maintain the rage, even though she probably *should*, but couldn't do it.

'Look, Alana,' she said, 'this isn't the time or the place to even be discussing this. I'm angry and you're upset and neither of us is making much sense any more. How about I accept your apology and we'll just let it go for now. OK?'

Alana sighed, the sound forlorn through the emptiness of the telephone wires. 'You're right, of course. And I *do* apologise, honestly. Not much wonder I'm off the wall; I barely slept all night. Probably,' she added grimly, 'the children. See you.'

And she was gone, hanging up quietly without waiting for Vashti's farewell.

Vashti hung up her own phone, but sat there, half expecting it to ring again, half tempted to ring Alana herself. It was ludicrous, she thought, for both of them to be feeling badly over what had been really no more than a childish prank, committed with the best of intentions.

'The road to hell is paved with good intentions,' she muttered at the silent telephone, then wished Alana a different path.

Vengeance, she thought, was fine for some people, but she wasn't one of them and didn't want to be. Then she found herself wondering about why Phelan hadn't answered *his* telephone when his sister rang. Any number of logical reasons filtered through her mind, but the only one that stuck was Alana's suggestion that perhaps he hadn't been there at all.

She had a mental flash of a leech with Janice Gentry's face, then forcibly ejected the image as unworthy. There had to be five thousand better reasons he hadn't answered his phone.

At least half of them rattled around like marbles in her skull, only to fly out of the window when he rapped on her door an hour later and she opened it to find him still in his clothes from the night before, looking just as he had at the start of the evening, except for his eyes.

'Don't even bother to say it; they look even worse from this side,' he said, ignoring a more conventional greeting. Vashti, wearing only faded jeans and a T-shirt, her hair crudely twisted up to keep it out of the way, could only stare at him.

'You look like death,' she said uncharitably. 'Are you sober?'

'As the proverbial judge,' he replied, and his grin was the same, flashing teeth that seemed rather at odds with those red-rimmed, ravaged eyes. 'I am prepared to swear that I've only had one alcoholic drink since I saw you last.'

'One drink, but no sleep, I presume,' she said, waving him inside, then rushing to steady him as he lurched across the lounge, collapsing on to the sofa, where he sprawled as if boneless.

'What *have* you been doing?' Vashti demanded. And had a flash of intuition. 'Surely not going off on the world's biggest ever guilt trip over the way you treated Alana last night? She phoned this morning— no, earlier this afternoon—worrying about you because she couldn't reach you.'

'Let her worry,' he sighed. 'Not that she was. All she was doing was checking to see where...no, whether...we were...if you know what I mean. Probably apologised profusely, as she ought. Knows she's still in deep trouble. Terrible child, my sister. Best of intentions, but a terrible child. Wants her bottom smacked.'

'She sounded reasonably contrite when she phoned,' Vashti said. 'And I think she was genuinely worried about you.'

'For goodness' sake, woman. I'm not a child—not even one of *her* children,' he said with a half-awake grin that didn't quite make it. 'Why in God's name should she be worried about my staying out all night? I don't live with her. I haven't even lived in the same house for about half her lifetime. She's never worried before; why should she start now?'

'Well, from the look of you, somebody should worry,' Vashti retorted. 'Do you want some coffee?'

'No coffee. Definitely no coffee. I've drunk enough coffee to float the QEII,' he muttered, somehow managing to sway even in his boneless, sagging slump. 'Just came to show you something. Unbelievable. All your fault, too, by the way. If anybody should be worried about me, it's you.'

Reaching, fumbling, he managed to get a hand into the inside pocket of his dinner-jacket. The hand stayed there; his eyelids slumped like empty sacks, then fluttered half open as his hand emerged with a piece of paper which he then waved expansively.

Vashti leaned down to pluck the paper from the air as he let it go, and straightened up to find herself holding a Wrest Point casino cheque for a quite incredible amount.

'Gambling? You've been up all night and half the day *gambling*?' She looked at Phelan, whose eyes had fallen closed again, then back at the cheque, which hadn't altered.

'Better than a cold shower,' he replied with what could have been a cheeky grin if he'd been awake enough to manage it. 'Takes longer, but——'

'You're mad as a meat axe,' she cried. And meant it. To have won this much, he must have risked, well, half that anyway. No sane person, she thought, could do that.

'Frustrated.' The word mumbled out of him as he slumped sideways to lie half sprawled on the sofa with his head hanging over the arm and his feet still on the floor.

Vashti looked at him, then found herself glancing wildly around the room and up to the ceiling as if there might be some deity to offer help. Fat chance!

'You can't go to sleep like that; you'll wake up as a pretzel,' she muttered, yanking at Phelan's arm to try to get him upright. Eyes like road-maps stared at her, unfocused, then he wobbled to his feet with her assistance and placidly allowed himself to be led into the bedroom, even to be propped against the wardrobe while she struggled to get his jacket off, then gripped him by the shoulders and swung him round to end up sitting on the edge of the bed.

'Nice,' he whispered as she knelt to unlace his shoes and remove them. Then was, thankfully, silent as she fumbled with his tie, irrelevantly noticing the crisp stubble on his chin as she did so.

And now? She drew a deep breath and started on the shirt studs, angrily slapping aside his fingers as he tried to manage them himself. She just couldn't give him a little push, topple him into her bed still wearing his clothes. But she wanted to; it would be safer.

He helped by falling over by himself once she had his shirt off, though it didn't make it much easier for her to relieve him of the trousers. She managed, finally, only too aware of the enforced intimacy involved.

'You're a worse nuisance than your sister,' she snarled, fighting the reaction she had to just lean down then and touch him. He was, she thought, quite splendid, his body muscular, lean almost to the point of gauntness. Crisp dark hair, not as coarse as that on his head, curled up from his groin to fan itself across his chest.

Just to look at him caused a *frisson* of emotion to run through her body, but it wasn't, Vashti realised, entirely sexual. Asleep now, his facial features had softened, regressed to the patterns of boyhood. He must, she thought, have been a happy child; even in sleep the lines around his eyes were laugh lines, and those surrounding his generous mouth were made by smiling.

Impulsively, she bent to touch his cheek, to kiss him ever so gently on the forehead. Then she carefully spread the feather quilt over him, picked up his clothes, and slipped out of the room. She hung up the dinner suit, suddenly totally embarrassed, incredibly aware of how he had looked, how he had felt, and the scent of him that still lingered on his shirt. She put the cheque back in the pocket from where he'd taken it, tucked his socks into his shoes and placed them neatly in the hall closet, then yielded to a sudden panic and rushed over to turn off the ringer on her phone.

For a moment she felt exhausted herself, though it had to be impossible since she'd slept most of the dozen hours that Phelan had spent gambling. Gambling! And this the man who'd told her he hardly ever gambled.

The man she now had to admit she wanted in her bed and had wanted there for some time. For all the good it does me, she thought, and wondered for a second if she was going to laugh or cry.

She frittered away most of the afternoon, dusting needlessly, tidying the already tidy, tiptoeing around like a little mouse to avoid making noise, and wondering quite astonishing things, like how Phelan Keene might react if he woke to find her beside him, or waiting here in the lounge in the lingerie she had to admit to herself she'd bought for *him* and which he'd never seen. She tried to read a book and failed, tried to do the *Sunday Tasmanian* crossword and failed even worse.

When would he wake up? And what would he do when he did? What would *she* do? What would they say? In the end, she gave it up, slipped out to her car, and drove over into Lenah Valley to the *Wursthaus*, where she spent half an hour in conversation with the butcher before finally choosing a selection of sausages—wallaby, hot Greek pork, various others— and a two-person leg of lamb. Over the road she found potatoes and other vegetables, buying an assortment, because she realised she had no idea of Phelan's taste in food. She struggled to remember what he'd eaten at the botanical gardens that time, but found the picture erased from her mind.

Ah, well, she thought, beggars can't be choosers, and laughed at the suggestion that a man with *that* cheque in his pocket might be considered a beggar. She drove home with the refrain of an old television commercial repeating in her mind—feed the man meat!

Her guest was still dead to the world when she peeked into the bedroom on her return, and she forced herself to work quietly as she prepared the meal, determined that the roast would be ready at seven, and, if he wasn't awake by then, he *would* be!

The simple, homely acts of cooking and setting the small kitchen table left her mind free to roam uninhibited, and Vashti was occasionally shocked and surprised with herself at the surprises she encountered while chilling the wine, while sneaking round to her neighbour's herb garden to pinch some fresh rosemary. She was not surprised, however, at the face she made when she went past the open bathroom and caught a glimpse of herself.

'Grotty,' she murmured, then had to stifle the laugh that came with her next thoughts. Sneaking into the bedroom, moving with the savage determination of a predator, she managed to emerge with what she'd gone for without Phelan even stirring.

Twenty minutes later, staring at her image in the mirror, she had second thoughts, but forced them away, thinking that Alana would have a fit if she could see Vashti, knowing Phelan's sister might have a fit anyway, if she knew where he was.

The old miniskirt, allegedly soon to become fashionable again, only just covered the tops of her stockings, and if she wasn't careful how she sat down the flimsy, frilly, *decadent* suspender belt was due for the exhibition she thought it had been intended for. Her blouse, this one neither old nor out of fashion, was of the softest jersey, and hugged her breasts with provocative innuendo, rather than being blatant. Just as well, she thought, having summoned up the courage—though only just!—to wear it without a bra.

Not wanting to risk the noise of a shower, she hadn't been able to wash her hair, hadn't really needed to since she'd done it during the sleepless hours of the night before, but she'd practically worn out her hairbrush to create a glossy, deliberately careless effect. A little make-up, but only a little, and dangly earrings completed the picture—just right, she thought, for the job of waking a slumbering prince.

She poured herself a glass of wine at six, another when the clock lied and said only ten minutes had passed. She checked the roast, checked it again, and argued with herself about whether to chicken out and put her bra on after all. Won. Or maybe lost, she thought with a self-satisfied grin, but left things as they were.

And at six-thirty precisely, she marched towards the bedroom, having liquefied her courage with a third glass of wine and still not sure it would be enough. She was standing there, hand raised to knock, her eyes closed as she summoned that last, vital bit of nerve, when the door opened a crack and one pale, still bloodshot eye peered out at her.

It looked her up and down; then a disembodied voice said, 'I see you're not wearing any trousers. Does that mean I can have them back? Or is this a come-as-you-are party?'

Flustered, she realised all his clothes were hung up in the hall closet, and if he emerged from the bedroom wearing what she left him in . . .

'Wait! Wait right there,' she cried. And rushed to grab up trousers and shirt, thrusting them through the crack in the door as if they were hot enough to burn her fingers. Maybe she only thought she heard a growl of laughter as the door closed. When it opened again she had her back turned, was kneeling to examine the roast, afraid to turn around, almost afraid to speak.

'Smells wonderful. Would there be time for me to steal a shower before we . . .?' The voice oozed chocolate fudge down her back; she could feel the warmth of it, tingled beneath the caress.

'Of course,' she said, rising easily to her full height without so much as a wobble of her stiletto heels. 'There are fresh towels in the cupboard and some of those throw-away razors in the medicine chest.'

She didn't dare turn around, poised as if for flight until she heard the bathroom door close and the sound of running water.

When he padded out to join her a few minutes later, hair close-kinked with moisture, and wearing only his trousers and shirt, sleeves casually rolled up, the first thing Vashti was aware of was how he looked at her.

It wasn't, as she had somehow expected—
wanted?—a survey of her provocative dress, nor even
a glance along the expanse of leg not covered by her
choice of skirt. He looked her square in the eye, his
own eyes still tired, but warm, friendly, comfortable.

'I'm not only a worse nuisance than my sister,' he
said, revealing he hadn't been *quite* asleep when she'd
removed his trousers, 'but I'm ruder as well. If I've
presumed by thinking I was invited to the feast you're
preparing, please just tell me to disappear and I'll try
to manage it as gracefully as I can.'

'You're invited,' Vashti replied, not quite sure how
to take *this* Phelan Keene. Did he think she'd be
planning a dinner party with him sleeping nearly
naked in her bed? Didn't he even notice the way she
was dressed? Was he even awake yet?

'I'll just put some shoes on, then,' he said. 'Can't
attend Sunday dinner barefoot, not with you looking
so delectable.'

Vashti poured him a glass of wine without asking
while he sank on to the sofa and put his socks and
shoes on, but suddenly found herself totally bereft of
any other social graces. She could only stand there
watching him, her mind empty of words, her uncertainty growing.

'Thank you,' he said when she handed him the
glass. 'And for the use of your bed, too. I have this
vague memory of just flaking out, but I imagine I
showed you that bloody great cheque, told you what
happened?'

'It's in the pocket of your jacket,' she said. 'And
no, you did *not* tell me what happened. Except that
you were gambling, which seemed obvious enough.

And gambling rather heavily, for somebody who claims not to indulge very often.'

'I wish you'd been there,' he replied with a grin. 'Although of course if you had been I wouldn't have dared punt like that, wouldn't even have been there, I suppose.'

'You're making no sense,' she replied. 'And please, sit down. You're making me nervous, hovering like that.'

'Do I recall you accusing me of getting a world-class guilt complex over how we messed with Alana?' he said, changing the subject as he turned a kitchen chair round and sat leaning on the back of it.

'I . . . may have said something like that,' Vashti replied, cautious now. Half asleep, Phelan was manageable; fresh from the shower, alert and wide awake, he was dangerous. 'I told you that she'd phoned here, looking for you, when she couldn't raise you at home.'

'I'll bet *that* impressed you,' he replied with a boyish grin. 'Bet you lied to her.'

'I did not. Why should I have? It was the middle of the day, for goodness' sake, no reason for you *not* to be here. And I wouldn't have lied anyway,' she said, doing exactly that. Then compounded it by adding, 'Not that it would have been necessary.'

'It should have been,' he said with a grin that was now positively wicked. 'Only my splendid sense of propriety saved you from being ravished last night. I'd give you a wonderful song and dance about how tragic it is to be so saintly and pure, except that I've already proved how lucrative it can be. And here I always thought virtue was its own reward.'

Vashti leaned back against the sink, twiddling her wine glass between her fingers. Carefully. The man was as egocentric as his sister, she told herself. Impossible.

'And what if you'd lost? I suppose you'd have just tried to write it off as research expenses?'

'Why,' he said, rising slowly from the chair and stalking over to stand in front of her, fencing her in with his arms after first setting down his own glass, then taking hers and doing the same, 'do I get the distinct impression you'd rather be a sex object than a research object?'

'Probably because that's all you ever have on your mind,' she snapped, ducking beneath his arm to the questionable freedom of a flat that suddenly seemed to shrink round the two of them. Phelan didn't pursue her; he assumed her earlier stance, leaning back comfortably as his eyes ranged over Vashti's tense figure.

'I'll bet you'd taste better than whatever it is you're cooking,' he said, licking his lips, already devouring her with his eyes. 'If you'd looked like that when I arrived, I wouldn't have been able to stay tired.'

'I've known teddy bears more dangerous than you were when you arrived,' she protested. 'And now, if you wouldn't mind getting out of the way, we might *both* have a chance to eat something tasty.'

'And if not?' He was being deliberately provocative now, but Vashti was getting wise to it.

'If not, the potatoes beside you will start boiling over and dinner will be ruined and it will all ... be ... your ... fault,' she said sternly. 'Now shift it! Go pour us some more wine while I finish up here.'

Phelan laughed, then turned and deftly shifted the pan of potatoes off to one side, lifting the lid as soon as the boil-over stopped. 'Another five minutes, at least,' he said. 'Would you like me to check the roast for you while I'm at it?'

'You can dish up, too, if you like,' she replied stubbornly, aware that if he so much as touched her, even if he was allowed to continue ravishing her with his eyes, dinner might as well go hang.

'I'd rather wash up, seeing I've managed to be so well behaved so far,' he said with a deprecating laugh. And moved aside, picking up the wine glasses as he did so.

Vashti poked at the potatoes with a long-handled fork, grudgingly admitting to herself that he'd been spot-on about the timing and equally aware that he'd hardly taken his eyes off her. She didn't have to turn and look; she *knew* he was watching, could actually feel him caressing her without even touching her.

And then he *was* touching her, and somehow she'd expected it, because she didn't drop the pan lid, didn't fly apart in a thousand pieces, or scream, or faint.

She merely turned under the guidance of his hands at her waist, turning to meet his descending lips with her own parted, welcoming, needing.

His fingers laced together round the small of her back, pulling her against him, fitting her to him as if she had been designed to fit just . . . so. Her own arms lifted, hands gathering behind his neck to hold him, to adjust the fit of his mouth against hers, feeling the coarse curls beneath her fingers, the warmth of his firm shoulder muscles against her wrists.

And it went on . . . and on . . . their breaths merging, the very flavours of them merging. She could smell him, the spicy, fresh-clean smell rich in her nostrils. As their tongues coiled together she tasted him, loving the taste, drinking it.

'Dinner later? Dinner now?' His voice was whisper-soft; he knew the answer, but was forcing her to say it, to admit it, to agree.

'Now,' she sighed into his mouth. But she *meant* later, and he knew that too. Keeping her prisoner with his lips, with one hand at her waist, he somehow reached out to turn knobs on the stove, to shut things off while he was turning her on.

'Now...dessert,' he whispered after a lifetime. And still claiming her mouth he lifted her, twisted her into the cradle of his arms, and carried her away from the kitchen and through the door to where the bed was still warm from his body.

CHAPTER EIGHT

VASHTI had to force herself at first. Her body screamed out for Phelan's caresses, seemed to fit itself so perfectly to him, to his touch. But her mind fitted the situation less well; it kept trying to interfere, to establish some sense, some order, some caution.

It would have been so easy to submit entirely, to simply abandon herself to the sensation that was heightened with his every caress. But she couldn't...quite. It was easy to have abandoned dinner, less easy to stop thinking about it. As his fingers raced patterns of delight along her spine, playing a sensuous symphony from buttocks to shoulders, as her own fingers explored his cheek, his neck, the touch of his lips against her own, she felt like a person divided.

And he didn't help. She wanted a swift and unthinking plunge into this unknown realm of their lovemaking, but Phelan by his slow, tortuous path forced her to take it step by step, touch by touch, sensation by sensation.

He plundered her mouth, but slowly, delicately, his kisses at times insistent, at times so teasing, so tantalisingly gentle, that she wanted to take the initiative herself, to roll him over so that she could dominate their lovemaking, force the pace herself.

His fingers touched her everywhere, moving across her cheeks like butterfly wings, spilling down across her neck and shoulders like warm water; his lips fol-

161

lowed, flooding her breasts with kisses, making the undoing of every blouse button a slow, deliberate adventure of delight. His fluttering touch along her ribcage only added to the wonder as he took each nipple in turn between his lips, making them firm, tender beyond all imagining.

Vashti twisted in his arms, wanting herself free of the now open blouse, wanting him free of his shirt, uanble to say what she wanted, unable to *say* anything. Her lips were buried in the hollow of his shoulder, her nostrils filled with the scent of him, her tongue flicking out like a snake's to taste him, to feel the texture of his skin, the bristling of beard at his throat.

Then she felt his mouth returning along her body, softly exploring between her breasts, laying tracks of kisses along her throat, returning to the home of her mouth, which awaited him desperately, eagerly.

His fingers lifted to free her of the constraining blouse; she had a half-felt sensation of it being stripped from her shoulders, flung away from them to sprawl unwanted, unneeded, somewhere beyond the world of the bed.

And as if guided by that action, her own hands lifted now to unravel the mystery of his shirt studs, so similar to buttons but so different. Her mind intruded, making pictures of how they worked, guiding her fingers so that the studs came free as easily as they had when she had taken the shirt from him earlier that day.

Her fingers now had freedom; they roved across the contours of muscle, the twisting patterns of the hair on his chest. Beneath them, his nipples hardened, firmed. She caught the soft gasp he uttered as her lips followed that path of exploration, and something inside her exulted at the reaction.

The tempo of their lovemaking quickened then. Their lips found each other to become the focus of the fusion that turned Vashti's entire body into a vessel of sensation. His fingers touched her spine and she quivered; they moved down along the line of her bottom, beyond the hampering fabric of the skirt to where those ever so expensive stockings only added to the smoothness of his caress.

Then back, blindly but quickly fumbling loose the fastenings of the skirt; her hips lifted, twisted, thrust against his manipulations. Her hand flew down to assist—was rejected, lifted away to find its own path along his chest and stomach.

Then the skirt was in flight, soaring after the blouse, to the sound of Phelan's appreciative groan, and her own gasp of delight as his lips fled from her mouth to scamper along the line of her breast, flickering across her stomach like swamp-fire, touching, branding, turning her body to jelly.

His fingers touched at her ankle, then she could *hear* the feel of them moving along her leg, their touch enhanced by the fine hosiery between his fingers and her skin. Until he reached to the top of the stocking; until his fingers and his lips met to ravage the warm softness of her inner thighs.

Vashti was contorted by the ecstasy of it. Her back arched; her hands flew to tangle themselves in his hair, holding his mouth against her, wanting the branding of his lips, hating the teasing of his tongue as it moved closer to the centre of her passion, then maddeningly away again.

'Beautiful ... soooo beautiful.' His voice, whisper-soft, became a litany that sang its way along her body, making her the instrument that accompanied the song. His fingertips lifted the music from her; his lips took the notes and shaped them, built them towards a crescendo, then slid away down the scale before she could catch up, teasing, tickling, tantalising.

She couldn't breathe, felt as if she never would again, gasped with each new sensation, each new and somehow different place his lips enlightened, each new part of her his knowing fingers explored. To the edge of oblivion and then away, back and forth and back again.

His mouth trekked across her body, climbing the hills and peaks, descending into secret valleys, finding oases of delight and leaving magic everywhere. His fingers found routes of their own, and they, also, dispersed magic. If she closed her eyes, it was to find sunbursts of sensation in her mind; open, it seemed the room was bathed in a wondrous light.

Vashti thought she might faint, was sure she could take no more, but wanted more and more and more. Wanted everything. Her hands crept along the muscles of his back and shoulders, the flat, hard planes of his hips, moving without conscious volition to fumble at the waistband of his trousers, to explore the throbbing warmth of him, touching, wondering, wanting him, all of him. Now.

Her flimsy knickers slid like oil from her body, giving way to his hands, his lips, as he stirred her body to a new awareness, yet another plateau of sensation. She gasped, heard herself moaning with pleasure beyond anything she had ever known, heard also his litany of compliments, of loving; she felt his body tense as if in agony, felt her own body writhing beneath his touch, crying out for his lips, his tongue.

His entrance was slow, almost teasingly so. She writhed beneath him, instictively trying to force the pace, to merge with him in totality. But he was stronger; he used his body, his hands, his lips in a symphony that took her to the brink of abandonment, held her there, teetering, until she could take no more. Then they plunged together into a time of magical union, melting into a single pool of sensation where it felt she could float forever.

And then she was in his arms, their bodies still united but her mind fuzzily seeking its way back to the real world, no longer conscious only of sensation, but able to see the man above her, to focus on his pale, strangely gentle eyes, able to feel his fingers as they touched her cheek, traced a pattern of love up the side of her nose, making that loving gesture of pushing up her non-existent glasses.

'My... God!' she sighed, staring up into those incredible eyes. And then, giving way to a sudden fit of shyness, she tucked her face in against his neck and was mute.

Phelan's hands moved along her back, holding her against him, holding them together, united now in a strangely peaceful union of both body and spirit.

As Vashti felt herself relaxing, his caresses slowly began to quicken, and she felt her body quicken in response even as her mind denied the possibility. Within her, he moved, filling her even further, rousing her slowly again to heights beyond belief, beyond even what they had shared before. This time they were together from the very moment of beginning, and Vashti's body seemed totally attuned to his rhythms, to the way he filled her, the way he moved within her, to his every touch, his every kiss.

This time when they plunged together it was as if they were a sky-diving team, but without parachutes, with no way to slow their descent into ecstasy, no need—because they were hand in hand, mouth to mouth, soul to soul. And at the end, no crashing arrival; it was light as the landing of a butterfly, and equally graceful.

'You are just sooo amazing,' he whispered, this time holding her gaze, banishing her need for shyness. 'I knew it would be like this.'

'How could you?' She met his eyes, reached up to touch his cheek, to move her fingers wonderingly along his lips. 'I . . . certainly didn't know.'

'I would have told you. Only we . . . sort of got off on the wrong foot.'

'I thought you hated me.' It had to come out; she had to *know*.

'Never that, but I did have some bloody awful mixed feelings,' he admitted. Still holding her, still meeting her eyes, still united.

'You thought I drove your father to the grave.' No question, this. She knew it; he knew it. Now it needed only an admission by both of them.

'I did, and the funny part is that I knew better, I think, right from the beginning. Only that was on an emotional basis, and you've had me so confused from the very beginning that I couldn't manage to think straight about it for the longest time.'

He kissed her then, his kiss a whisper of security, of promise, then eased himself gently away so that he was able to prop himself on one elbow, looking down at her while his fingers moved to caress her breasts.

'Writers sometimes aren't the most rational of people,' he said. 'Too much emotion and not enough plain common sense.'

Vashti wriggled under his touch, feeling like a puppy being stroked. And loving every instant, every sensation.

'I talked to the old man a few days before he died,' Phelan explained, 'and he mentioned the audit, said it was shaping up to be a proper mishmash, and that he was really worried about it, because he wasn't a tax cheat, never had been, but was afraid he was going to come out looking like one.'

'He wasn't,' Vashti said, reaching down to halt the progress of his insidious fingers. 'He wasn't any sort of tax cheat, and I knew it and he knew I knew it. I can't imagine why he'd say such a thing.'

'He'd been drinking a bit, and he was just upset enough that he rambled, couldn't seem to keep all the bits and pieces of the story in any logical order,' Phelan said. 'And not knowing it all from the beginning, I had a lot of trouble following the thread.'

Disentangling her fingers, he returned his hand to her breast, then moved it lower, slowly tracing circles until he reached where his touch could destroy any hope of concentration. Vashti moved to stop him, then gasped and thrust herself against the pressure, yielding to his touch, all thought gone except that of the sensations he roused in her body.

'Not . . . fair,' she sighed some time later. 'How can you expect me to pay attention when you're doing that?'

'It's a long explanation,' he replied with a truly wicked grin. 'I wouldn't want you to get bored.'

Vashti matched his grin, her hand lifting to touch his lips, then moving down along the length of his body, tweaking at his nipples, then seeking the most obvious form of retaliation, revelling in her power as he stiffened in reply.

'You were saying?'

His answer now was to loom over her, seeking her mouth with his own, letting her guide him to his goal, then taking control so that she had no choice but to follow him back to the edge of ecstasy, her body his to plunder, to pleasure, to possess.

'I was saying,' he continued much, much later, 'that Dad ended up pretty upset, and the last thing he said was something about "that damned woman". Then the line dropped out, for some reason, and . . . I never talked to him again.'

Sadness flowed in to replace the loving in his eyes, and Vashti reached up to touch his face, to somehow comfort him. He smiled his acceptance, fingers reaching to hold her own.

'But of course when I got to the funeral and saw you, I thought . . . well, you can imagine what I thought. I hadn't talked to Bevan or Alana about you at that point, and even when we did discuss the whole issue of your audit . . . I was already blind and I stayed that way. Even though it was obvious both of them liked you.'

He reached down and shifted the down coverlet over them, using the gesture to let him then hide from view the movements of his hand as he returned it to caress her thighs above the stockings. Vashti tightened against his probing fingers, holding him still between her thighs, shaking her finger in a 'halt' gesture they both knew to be powerless.

'I knew that,' she said, 'although I didn't realise it until...until...'

'Until *that* woman—the one the old man really meant when he said it—accused you. That's when I took a good look at myself and realised what an utter fool I'd been,' Phelan said. 'Worse than a fool—a damned, blind idiot. I could have killed the bitch, right there on the spot. Except that I was just so...so angry with *myself* as well, that I didn't know which to do first—murder her or come grovelling to you.'

'It wouldn't have mattered,' Vashti said. 'I was just so stunned, so *hurt*, that I wouldn't have listened. I *didn't* listen.'

'Well, you didn't make it easy for me to explain; that's for sure. And I was so damned confused myself about it all that I was probably coming on a bit heavy. I won't even apologise for that, although probably I should. You just got under my skin from the very first moment I saw you. Even the way I felt then, I could barely keep my hands off you.'

'It's called "lust" in some books by authors who shall remain nameless,' she replied cheekily. 'And keep that hand still if you want to continue this conversation.'

'Plenty of time,' he grinned. 'It isn't as if we have to leap out of this bed and go anywhere. We could, indeed, stay here for days and days. We've got food, wine...'

'Even a loaf of bed. Stop that!' she cried, then joined him in laughing at the Freudian slip. 'And I have a job to go to tomorrow, in case you've forgotten. My boss—by some miracle I shall never understand—gave me half of Friday off; he'd be just a bit hostile if I didn't make it in on time tomorrow.'

'Phone him first thing in the morning and say you're still in bed,' Phelan chuckled, moving *that* hand just enough to divert her attention. 'I'll make damned sure it won't be a lie.'

'You will not!'

'I probably wouldn't have the strength,' he said. 'All this *lust* has made that lamb roast look better than you do, almost. I don't suppose you'd like to stop fondling my body long enough to get back in the kitchen?'

'Wearing just what I'm wearing, I suppose?' she replied with a grin, all thought of shyness long gone. 'Or do I at least get to put on an apron?'

'I should certainly hope so,' he said, swinging out of the bed and reaching down to lift her to stand beside him. 'No way am I going to let you put this body at risk. It has a lot of years of good value left in it.'

Twenty minutes later—both wearing at least *something*—they sat across from each other at the kitchen table, demolishing Vashti's roast dinner as if neither had eaten for weeks.

'I'm pleased you're a good cook,' Phelan said, teasingly. 'Being sexy and decorative is all right in its place, but when all is said and done...'

'You mean that's all there was?' Vashti could tease too, she found, and revelled in it. 'I'd have thought your hero's abilities were more than just wishful thinking.'

'You're starting to sound like my sister,' he cautioned. 'Keep it up and I won't help with the dishes, much less phone in your excuses in the morning.'

'No such thing,' she said, eyes widening at what she imagined Ross Chandler's reaction would be to a telephone call from one of her clients saying she was in bed and couldn't come to work. Then she giggled, unable not to at the mental picture she'd created.

'All right, I suppose it wouldn't be the best idea,' he admitted with a chuckle of his own. 'I will do the dishes, though, provided you promise to keep your hands off my body. Any fondling and you'll be picking up broken crockery for the next fortnight.'

'You can dry,' she said. 'No, on second thoughts, *I'll* dry. You'd only take advantage of me while I had both hands in the sink. This way, I keep control, and besides, I know where everything goes. You can tell me all about your gambling foray while you're at it.'

Which he proceeded to do in great detail, creating for Vashti a wonderful, hilarious story; she howled so much at one point that she almost started dropping dishes herself.

'Oh, I wish I'd been there,' she cried, only to have Phelan flick a fistful of suds at her.

'I've already told you—if you'd been there I wouldn't have done it,' he said with a mock-scowl. 'Because if we'd been together, we'd have been *here*, and there'd have been other things on my mind besides gambling, I can tell you that!'

'We were here,' she said, serious for a moment. 'And you did have other things on your mind. But you didn't stay.'

'I did not!'

'Why not?'

'Because it wouldn't have been right.'

'You can say that, now? I...don't think I understand.'

'You were too tired to understand anything,' he replied, 'which is why I didn't stay. And, I suppose, why I came back today, if you want the truth.'

'Of course I do. This isn't one of your books, for goodness' sake.'

'Sometimes I wonder. When life starts getting stranger than my own fiction, well . . .'

'I . . . I really would like to know,' she said hesitantly, afraid now she was about to get an answer she didn't want to hear.

Phelan grinned, the sheer magic of his grin dispelling the worst of her fears.

'You were too tired,' he said again. 'The timing was wrong, the circumstances were wrong, everything was wrong. It would have been a disaster. And—you would have hated me in the morning.'

'I wouldn't!'

'You might have. *I* might have.' His eyes flashed for an instant, radiating something Vashti couldn't quite discern.

'And besides,' he said in a tone of voice just a tinge different somehow, 'when I left here last night I was broke, or near as damn it.' His eyes were on what he was doing in the sink now; Vashti could only hear what he was saying, not see his expression.

'And you thought that would matter to me?'

Her voice must have registered some of the confusion she felt, the astonishment.

'It would have mattered to me. One doesn't take advantage of a beautiful woman when one can't even afford to offer to buy her breakfast afterwards.'

Vashti could only laugh.

'And last night I was feeling . . . lucky,' he continued, pretending not to notice. 'Probably because of what I *now* think might have been misplaced feelings about being virtuous and honourable and all that stuff. Not realising what a wanton you really are, I had myself convinced that it would have been wrong to take advantage, so even before we left the casino I was busy talking myself out of my lustful ideas. Which I did, and I left here feeling quite pleased with myself.

'Now, of course,' he said with a mischievous grin, 'I realise I was only lucky you didn't trip me and beat me to the floor. But I couldn't have known that then, could I? Not when I was busy convincing myself not to work my wicked way with you because . . . I wanted it to be right. More than right, damn it! Perfect!'

'You're not making a lot of sense,' Vashti said, picking up the cutlery all in a bunch and drying the bits as they came to hand.

'More than you do, sometimes,' he said, reaching down to stop her. 'Are you trying to cut off a finger or something?'

'Don't be silly,' she replied. 'I do this all the time.'

'Well, don't do it when I'm around, OK? I don't want the body damaged; it's far too valuable.'

'Just get on with your story,' she said. 'I'm still waiting for the full explanation. And . . . I have a knife in my hand now. So be truthful.'

'I was afraid you'd insist on that,' he replied. 'Anyway, knowing I was going to be virtuous—presuming I got the chance to have a choice—I saved out one chip from the lot I cashed in to give me an excuse.'

'An excuse for what?'

'For not taking advantage, of course. That way I could convince myself I ought to be virtuous because you'd brought me luck and I still had *your* chip in my pocket, so I'd have to go back and finish up that run of luck.'

'Have you been reading your own books or something?' Vashti cried. 'That's the most convoluted, nonsensical load of old cobblers I've ever heard.'

'I was looking after your best interests,' he replied, totally unabashed. Except for that wicked gleam in his eyes.

'And what would you have done, pray tell, if I'd come on all frisky? What if I *had* tripped you and beaten you to the floor, as you so politely put it?'

'I'd have helped!'

'And then what?'

'Probably borrowed the money from you to buy you breakfast—is that what you want to hear?' His scowl was fierce, but his eyes were warm, laughing.

I want to hear you say you love me! The words flashed through her mind in huge, blazing capital letters. But went unsaid. Instead, she resorted to cheekiness, taking solace from the fact that she was comfortable enough with Phelan to allow that much.

'Maybe I just want to hear you say you've finished the washing-up,' she said. 'It would be awfully hard to trip you while you can grab the sink for support.'

'You're insatiable, woman,' he accused with a grin. 'I'm going as fast as I can and it still isn't good enough for you. I might have to change my mind about this whole arrangement; I can't have a heroine with such lustful ideas in a romance. The research would kill me before I could manage to finish the damned thing.'

'And that's what I am? A heroine for one of your books?' Vashti couldn't meet his eyes, could hardly credit her own daring, didn't *want* to. Nor did she want to hear the answer, but it was too late now!

'Is that what you think?'

He smiled, but it was a false smile, a liar's smile. She *knew* it was, suddenly hated him. Hated herself more. Wanted to run, but couldn't, of course. This was her home; this was where she ought to be running to, not from. And in that burning instant the wonder of the afternoon seemed to collapse around her. Impossible, she thought, but she tasted deception where she'd only tasted love, caring.

'For the book you're working on now? The one about the tax office? That's what it's all been about, isn't it? You've just been *using* me.' She was becoming hysterical, could hear it in her own voice, could see it in the strange look on Phelan's face, the stranger light in his eyes.

'Well? Is that it? It is—isn't it? *Isn't* it?'

She was screaming at him now, waving the knife she'd forgotten she even held until just that instant. '*Isn't it*? This whole damned thing has been nothing more than a...a charade, a game, to you. You've been orchestrating it all with that...*that* woman, *just for a lousy book*!'

'I don't believe this.'

He was reaching out, braving the knife to lift the tea-towel from her other hand, using it to wipe the soap suds from his hands. And all the while looking at her, shaking his head in tiny, abrupt motions.

'Answer me!'

He reached out, plucked the knife from her fingers, and flung it into the sink. The gesture was swift, angry.

But his eyes weren't angry. Only...different, somehow.

'Will you please come and sit down?'

'*No*! I want an answer and I want it *now*!'

Phelan sighed, looking down at the floor for an instant, his shoulders drooping.

'Please?'

'*Now*, damn you.'

'All right,' he said, voice quiet, resigned. 'Yes, I'm writing a book. That *is* what I do...write books. And yes, it's about the tax office, sort of. But I am not— repeat *not*—using you. Nor am I *using* whatever tax affairs were between us.'

He paused, looked in her eyes and saw the fury, the hurt, the total disbelief, and sighed again.

'And I don't know how you could think I would.'

Not one word about Janice Gentry, not even a suggestion of denial about his involvement with her, their pictures together in the paper, her obvious attitude to him.

'You're lying.' She fought to control her growing hysteria, made the statement flat, emotionless.

Phelan just looked at her, eyes weary, but cold now. He shook his head.

'OK,' he said then, 'I guess you're entitled to your opinion, no matter how ridiculous it is.'

Without waiting for a reply, he stepped around her, quickly gathering up shoes and socks, and shrugging into his shirt. He took his dinner-jacket from the hall closet as he passed it, and walked out of the door.

He didn't slam it, didn't even look back as he slouched down the footpath in his bare feet, climbed into his luxury motor car, and drove slowly, almost sedately, out of her life.

Vashti watched him go without a tear, then plunged into the shower and stayed there, trembling and shivering in the steam, scrubbing him away. Obsessively, compulsively, angrily. Fruitlessly. Until the hot water turned cold.

CHAPTER NINE

'THE Keene file is closed!'

Vashti blurted out the words and could have kicked herself for how she knew they sounded. Ross Chandler didn't appear to notice, any more than he'd noticed that she was half an hour late for work.

'All right,' he said, lifting his small, shrewd eyes from the mountain of paperwork on his desk only long enough to utter those two words.

'I've ... I ... it just shouldn't have been me,' Vashti stammered, then plunged on. 'The audit is complete now anyway and there's no evidence against ... Mr Keene.'

'I said it was all right.' He didn't even bother to look up this time. He'd seen her come into his office, dressed appropriately for a businesswoman, hair neatly spun into a chignon, tailored skirt and jacket, sensible shoes. If he'd noticed the vain attempt to disguise reddened eyes and a complexion pale as death, he didn't bother to say.

'I'm ... sorry. It's the first time ...' Vashti couldn't just accept *his* acceptance; she felt she must try and explain, *had* to somehow explain. Only she couldn't, couldn't even get the words together sufficiently to make a coherent sentence.

He looked up again, impatient now. She knew the signs, had seen them often enough before. And now, she realised, he was noticing her appearance.

'I said it didn't matter, Vashti,' he said, unusually gentle for the mood she could see he was in. 'Why don't you go home? You look worse than you did on Friday.'

I looked *fine* on Friday, she wanted to scream. Infinitely better than now! A million times better than now! And I felt better, too.

'I'm fine,' was all she could manage. 'Just . . . tired, a bit. But I didn't sleep in or anything; I was late because my car played up and wouldn't start, so I had to walk.'

'If you're so fine, you might explain why you charged into the building—admittedly late, but let's ignore that—and promptly went off to be sick?'

'How . . . ?' She had to stop, or risk being sick again.

'I know everything. That's why I'm the boss.' And he bent again to his paperwork. 'Now either go on back to work or book yourself off sick, but stop standing around my office like a dog waiting to be shot.'

He didn't know everything, *couldn't* know everything, thank God, she thought as she fled back to the relative sanctuary of her own office, moving fairly stiffly, as if all her muscles were sore, knowing why and hating it, hating even more the way all her nerve-endings seemed exposed, tender. It was like the worst of hangovers without the headache.

Only hangovers, she decided a week later, didn't go on and on, *ad infinitum*, didn't renew themselves without a fresh infusion of what started them, didn't creep up unseen to leap out of the bushes at one with no warning, no chance of defence.

She had read something once about the so-called 'drinker's hour', that apparently horrific time in the wee small hours when alcoholics woke to sweats and nightmares and unknown, unseen, indescribable fears. Did they also, she wondered, have insanely erotic nightmares?

Worse, did they have them in the middle of the day, in the middle of walking down a city street where a glint of glossy dark hair, a certain type of masculine posture, a certain type of walk, could make one go weak at the knees, could create a dryness in the mouth, a moist, spongy feeling in the tummy?

By the end of another week, she had generally stopped finding herself assaulted by such feelings while at work, where it was damnably embarrassing to be recalled to the present and find herself squirming in her seat, her body burning, her clothing insanely constricting.

But it was done now. Finished. Over. Had been for days when Vashti got the call from downstairs asking if a Miss Alana Keene might be allowed to see her without an appointment.

'No,' she replied instinctively, only to relent within the space of a heartbeat. Her calendar was a desert; she could spare three hours without any appointment if she wanted to. Which she damned well didn't, but couldn't in all conscience find a single excuse even *she* would think worthy. And she liked Alana, despite the girl's propensity for meddling, despite her...relatives.

Alana walked through the door a few moments later, granting Vashti a fleeting smile, but having little else in her demeanour that indicated friendliness.

'I am instructed,' she said gravely, 'to deliver this to you personally, by hand, and—if possible—to obtain a receipt.'

'This' was a fat, large *Jiffy bag* which Alana was holding as if it contained live tiger-snakes. She plunked the parcel down on Vashti's desk with obvious relief, took a deep breath, and announced dramatically, 'And I am instructed to sit here while you read it.'

'Alana, the audit is over, all done, finished,' Vashti said. 'I don't see——'

'Exactly my point,' Alana interrupted. 'You don't see, and without a bit of help you probably never will. Now will you please just humour me and read this so I can finish my penance and get back to what passes for a normal life again?' The girl's tension was unnerving, and it forced her voice up and up and up with every word. She was almost screaming at the end.

'Must I?' Stupid question, Vashti realised, as Alana stomped over to sit down beside the window, glaring at her, tense, angry, defensive. It would have something to do with Phelan; Vashti was certain of it, and even more certain when Alana snapped,

'Too right you do!'

'You wouldn't like to leave it with me and we can talk about it over lunch?' Vashti ventured, seeking some semblance of sweet reason, some escape valve for the naked hostility that filled the office like smoke.

'I am instructed to *watch* you read it. Every... single... word! If possible,' she added, making it obvious she wasn't impressed with even that concession.

'Dare I ask what penance you're talking about?' Vashti asked gently. Very gently! Alana was clearly upset, and Vashti didn't want to make it any worse.

'That,' her visitor replied, 'is a very, very silly question. Please, Vashti... will you just *read* the damned thing and stop harassing me? I've been harassed quite enough over this already and I'm getting intensely sick of it.'

Alana sighed as if she could see the end of the world, then leaped to her feet and rushed forward. 'Please,' she pleaded, hostility exchanged now for concern. 'I'm sorry I played at being a matchmaker; I'll never do it again as long as I live, I swear it! All I wanted was for you and Phelan to stop being stupid and get it together; it isn't *my* fault that . . . whatever happened.' And she sighed hopelessly. 'But I can't handle this being an . . . an intermediary, either. I *told* him that, but *he* said I owed him—owed *both of you*. Please.'

The final plea was so genuine, so heart-breaking, that Vashti couldn't refuse, despite her better judgement.

'All right,' she said. 'But I'd rather be alone.'

Alana closed her eyes, obviously on the brink of agreeing, but her courage failed her. Shaking her head, she walked slowly back to her chair and slumped in it, quite obviously prepared to sit and stare at the floor, if necessary, until Vashti had read whatever it was she was supposed to read.

'At least take this,' Vashti sighed, reaching into her bottom drawer for the Dick Francis novel she was currently involved in. 'I won't be able to concentrate on anything with you sitting there sighing like some spectre of doom.' She tossed the paperback over to Alana, who looked at it as if it were a cheese sandwich or something, sighed again, and nodded some vague form of agreement.

There was a note attached to the bulky manuscript that emerged from the Jiffy bag.

I wanted to be sure you'd read this, and couldn't wait a year or more for it to be published first. So I'm sending it in manuscript form—at great cost for the photocopying of same. My sister the former matchmaker has strict instructions to *watch* you read it, and if you refuse she is to knock you down, sit on you, and *read it aloud*, if necessary. I suggest you take the easy way out.

Vashti snarled aloud and glared over to where Alana was peeeping over the top of the paperback, so alert that she *almost* managed to duck her head without Vashti catching her at it.

It was an incident that occurred and recurred with ludicrous regularity over the next hour and a half as Vashti forced her way through the manuscript, at first skimming quickly, then making heavier work of it as she became lost—at least occasionally—in the story itself.

Phelan Keene's tax book. His tax *romance*. And yes, the heroine was blonde, small, with grey eyes... and *glasses*... and a tiny mole where the author shouldn't have known it was! Her involuntary gasp at that disclosure brought, she was sure, a muffled giggle from behind the paperback, but her stern glance revealed no eyes peeping over the top.

And yes, the owner of those eyes was in the book, too, fat ankles and all. That brought a chuckle from Vashti herself, but she must have stifled it well because once again she failed to catch Alana out.

And, Vashti had to admit, there wasn't one thing about the tax office or its workings that Phelan couldn't have found out just by picking up a phone and asking. Much less was there anything he might have gained through *using* her.

The romance part, however, was something else again. As was the entire interplay between hero and heroine. All of that, she recognised. Every word, every nuance, every touch, every kiss, every emotion. Even the kitchen knife.

As she read, she felt at first as if her entire relationship with Phelan had been conducted in a glasshouse, or in front of a movie camera, to be exhibited to the world. Her stomach churned; she had to swallow several times to keep from being physically sick. But gradually she realised that *his* emotions, too, were just as revealed, just as obvious. To everybody, it seemed, but her!

And his heroine, to her astonishment, emerged as a wonderfully well-rounded person—a private person, to be sure, but a true *heroine*, who faced problems and conquered them, who was anything but the sex-object doormats he'd portrayed in his other books.

When she finally reached the dénouement, the part where hero and heroine resolved their differences and figuratively rode off into the sunset together, she had to stop. She was certain for a long, eyes-closed moment that she couldn't go on. Didn't dare.

Forgotten were her divided feelings at finding it all there, all written down for her to review—the love-making, the Japanese bridge, the roast lamb dinner!— all there to be forced upon her, to *make* her see his side of it, to see aspects of her *own* side of it that she hadn't been aware of.

She wanted to know how it ended, but didn't dare keep reading. Stop at the end of chapter eight. Stop and don't ever dare read further, she vowed. It will surely destroy you, destroy everything!

Slyly glancing up to make sure Alana was still in hiding behind the book, Vashti turned over the last chapter unread, and gathered the manuscript together with what she hoped would give an appearance of having finished it. Then she grabbed up a piece of scrap paper and scrawled a receipt, dashing off the words in an almost unreadable flurry of chicken-tracks.

'You can come out now,' she said, knowing her voice was furry, trembling. Like her body. 'I'm done and I haven't exploded yet.'

Violet eyes, moist with concern, peered over the top of the book. Then a face emerged, but there was no smile, only a rather grimly determined stare. Alana got up and moved cautiously over to exchange the paperback for the receipt, then walked with equal caution over to the door.

'You didn't finish,' she called back over her shoulder. 'You didn't read the final chapter.'

Vashti couldn't lie, but couldn't admit it, either. Alana didn't even wait for a reply.

'I know because you're still here, dummy!' she cried. 'Damn it, Vashti. He loves you. L.O.V.E.S. What do you want him to do—grovel?'

She swung open the office door and stepped out, then back, holding the door open as she scowled fiercely. 'If we weren't friends I wouldn't say this,' she snarled. 'But sometimes you are just too...*strong* for your own good.' And she slammed the door behind her.

Vashti hardly noticed. She sat there, staring into space, into memory and the past and the future at the same time, for the longest time. Then she turned over the manuscript and started again from the beginning, not skimming this time but reading each and every word, right through to the end of chapter eight, and then, before she could talk herself out of it, on into the unknown.

On to where he ripped up the cheque for his gambling winnings, took the heroine in his arms, and declared, 'The best things in life aren't free—they're shared. I love you, and if I can't share my life with you it isn't hardly worth bothering with. I love you, and I'll wait forever if I have to.'

Ross Chandler looked up in surprise when she knocked on his door and strode into the office without waiting for his bark of admittance.

'I'm taking the rest of the day off,' she declared. 'I'll make it up some time later.'

She didn't wait for his answer either. The taxi she'd called would be downstairs by now.

Twenty minutes later she was on the road in her own car, crossing the Bridgewater causeway, and turning up the Boyer Road with all her senses alert; this was no time to be taking risks. Not now.

She held to the speed limit, only too aware it was far slower than the screaming pace in her heart and mind. New Norfolk, Hamilton, Ouse, all passed in a haze as she concentrated only on the ribbon of highway in front of her. What she passed was irrelevant; her destination was the only thing of importance now.

The tiny church was in sunshine, this day, crouched snugly beneath its sentry pines in a quiet that held its own sound. He rose from the stoop as she skidded to a halt in the gravel turnaround, was smiling, arms outstretched to gather her in as she flew through the gate.

His auburn hair blazed in the sunshine, and his eyes held a special glow of their own, a glow that not even sunshine could produce, because it came from within.

Vashti stepped from her car, feeling an instant's hesitation, a flicker of caution that she flung from her like an intruding insect. Irrelevant!

She had her priorities right now, and she knew it as she marched straight into arms that closed round her slender waist, lifting her to meet his smiling lips.

'If you tore up that cheque, I'll kill you,' she cried when he finally released her mouth, when her heart had slowed down enough to allow speech of any kind. 'I'm going to have to borrow from it to pay Alana for the tickets.'

'What tickets?' he asked after kissing her again so thoroughly that she was sure he hadn't heard.

'The theatre tickets, the night...you know!'

'Ah...*that* night.' And his grin was infectious. 'The night of the second-biggest gambling win of my life. You don't *really* think I'd have ripped up that cheque? Not really?'

'What do you mean, second-biggest win?' she countered, visibly sighing with relief not because she cared about the money—it was irrelevant despite the amount—but because she didn't, *couldn't* accept herself as the cause of throwing that much away, like in the book. Damned book, wonderful, wonderful book! The best book, the most important book she would ever read, Vashti knew. And was glad of it.

Phelan's first answer was silent, his mouth capturing hers in a reply that was none the less clear.

Vashti could only accept, her nostrils filled with the scent of him, his touch like lightning wherever his fingers traced intricate, intimate designs along her body. She reached up to touch his face, to run her fingers along the strong column of his neck, into the thatch of hair at his nape. Her toes still touched the ground, although only just, but that was enough; elsewhere their bodies seemed to meld into one, each part fitting against the other in a splendid blend of rightness.

'I love you, you know?' was his second reply. 'But I'd never make it as a writer if I couldn't tell the difference between fiction and real life.

'Today was the biggest gamble, by far. And *this* is the biggest win.' His fingers crept along her spine, playing an ancient tune that sent music right to her soul.

'For both of us,' she sighed, trying to move closer into his arms and knowing it wasn't possible here. Having to let go of him, to have him let go of *her*, so they could get into separate vehicles just to remedy that situation was like walking into winter. Thankfully, it was short-lived.

They were considerably closer in the bed at the ancient farmhouse when he finished kissing her for the thousandth time and said, 'I may give up gambling now. I think I've found a much more pleasant pastime.'

'Good,' she said. 'This is much healthier for you.' And her exploring fingers revealed just how *much* healthier. Phelan seemed suitably impressed.

'Just as addictive. Maybe more,' he sighed as she reached a particularly sensitive spot.

'I should hope so.'

The conversation lapsed for a time, at least in verbal terms, but eventually Phelan slowed the pace sufficiently to allow him breath to speak.

'You can't pay Alana for those tickets, by the way. Did she *really* ask you to?'

'Sort of,' Vashti replied, her mind barely on the conversation, far too engrossed in what his hands were doing while he spoke. 'Why can't I pay her?'

'Because you have to pay *me*. *I'm* the one who bought them; she shouldn't benefit just because I didn't ask you, didn't think you'd go. So I gave them to her—*gave*—and only agreed to go myself when she rang at the last minute and said she couldn't find anybody to go with and didn't want to go alone. All trickery, and now she expects to be paid, the devious little bitch. I'll put her in a book—that'll fix her!'

'Just don't forget the fat ankles,' Vashti sighed, then gave herself to the magic of his fingers. Literally.

Accept 4 FREE Romances and 2 FREE gifts

FROM READER SERVICE

Here's an irresistible invitation from Mills & Boon. Please accept our offer of 4 FREE Romances, a CUDDLY TEDDY and a special MYSTERY GIFT! Then, if you choose, go on to enjoy 6 captivating Romances every month for just £1.80 each, postage and packing FREE. Plus our FREE Newsletter with author news, competitions and much more.

Send the coupon below to: Mills & Boon Reader Service, FREEPOST, PO Box 236, Croydon, Surrey CR9 9EL.

NO STAMP REQUIRED

Yes! Please rush me 4 FREE Romances and 2 FREE gifts! Please also reserve me a Reader Service subscription. If I decide to subscribe I can look forward to receiving 6 brand new Romances for just £10.80 each month, post and packing FREE. If I decide not to subscribe I shall write to you within 10 days - I can keep the free books and gifts whatever I choose. I may cancel or suspend my subscription at any time. I am over 18 years of age.

Ms/Mrs/Miss/Mr _____ EP55R

Address _____

_____

Postcode _____ Signature _____

Offer closes 31st March 1994. The right is reserved to refuse an application and change the terms of this offer. One application per household. Overseas readers please write for details. Southern Africa write to Book Services International Ltd., Box 41654, Craighall, Transvaal 2024.
You may be mailed with offers from other reputable companies as a result of this application. Please tick box if you would prefer not to receive such offers ☐

mps
MAILING
PREFERENCE
SERVICE

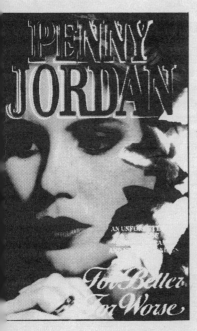

Next Month's Romances

Each month you can choose from a wide variety of romance with Mills & Boon. Below are the new titles to look out for next month, why not ask either Mills & Boon Reader Service or your Newsagent to reserve you a copy of the titles you want to buy – just tick the titles you would like and either post to Reader Service or take it to any Newsagent and ask them to order your books.

Please save me the following titles: **Please tick** | ✓

Title	Author	
HEART OF THE OUTBACK	Emma Darcy	
DARK FIRE	Robyn Donald	
SEPARATE ROOMS	Diana Hamilton	
GUILTY LOVE	Charlotte Lamb	
GAMBLE ON PASSION	Jacqueline Baird	
LAIR OF THE DRAGON	Catherine George	
SCENT OF BETRAYAL	Kathryn Ross	
A LOVE UNTAMED	Karen van der Zee	
TRIUMPH OF THE DAWN	Sophie Weston	
THE DARK EDGE OF LOVE	Sara Wood	
A PERFECT ARRANGEMENT	Kay Gregory	
RELUCTANT ENCHANTRESS	Lucy Keane	
DEVIL'S QUEST	Joanna Neil	
UNWILLING SURRENDER	Cathy Williams	
ALMOST AN ANGEL	Debbie Macomber	
THE MARRIAGE BRACELET	Rebecca Winters	

If you would like to order these books in addition to your regular subscription from Mills & Boon Reader Service please send £1.90 per title to: Mills & Boon Reader Service, Freepost, P.O. Box 236, Croydon, Surrey, CR9 9EL, quote your Subscriber No:..................................... (If applicable) and complete the name and address details below. Alternatively, these books are available from many local Newsagents including W.H.Smith, J.Menzies, Martins and other paperback stockists from 12 March 1994.

Name:..

Address:...

....Post Code:..........................

To Retailer: If you would like to stock M&B books please contact your regular book/magazine wholesaler for details.

You may be mailed with offers from other reputable companies as a result of this application. If you would rather not take advantage of these opportunities please tick box   ☐